Jessica Haggerthwaite:
Media Star

Jessica Haggerthwaite:
Media Star

Emma Barnes

illustrated by
Tim Archbold

BLOOMSBURY
CHILDREN'S
BOOKS

First published in Great Britain in 2003 by Bloomsbury Publishing Plc,
38 Soho Square, London W1D 3HB

A CIP record of this book is available from the
British Library

ISBN 0 7475 5911 2

Printed in Great Britain by Clays Ltd, St Ives plc

10 9 8 7 6 5 4 3 2 1

For Rosy, officially best sister in the world – EB

To Louise, Rosie and John – TA

Chapter One

If there was one thing Jessica Haggerthwaite could not stand, it was a quiet life. Plenty of other things drove her mad too: hearing people ask 'What's it like having a witch for a mother?' for the eighty-fifth time, for example ('Absolutely dreadful,' she would reply); or being called Jessie instead of Jessica; or sitting through geography lessons. But at the end of the day, nothing drove her quite so mad, quite so quickly, as being bored.

'Nothing ever happens around here,' she complained to her brother Midge, thumping her bag against the railings as they walked home from school.

'What do you mean?' asked Midge indignantly. 'Have you forgotten being in the *Bellstone Gazette*?

You went on about it for days. Or winning that science competition? And don't bang your bag like that. It frightens Liverwort.'

Liverwort, the Haggerthwaites' pet toad, was travelling on Midge's shoulder. He gave a worried croak.

'See?' said Midge. 'He's terrified!'

'He is not,' said Jessica. 'He has insufficient brain to be frightened.'

'He does not! And he's frightened of lots of things! Cats and thunderstorms and the piano in assembly.

'Yes, and that's exactly why you should let him stay safe at home in his tank.' (Midge, who knew this perfectly well, said nothing.) 'Anyway, when I said nothing ever happens, I meant nothing *recently*.'

Midge gave a sigh of exasperation. Sometimes, he could not understand his sister. She might be older than him in years, but sometimes he felt she was much younger when it came to plain common sense.

Personally, Midge liked a quiet life. It was just a shame that, with a sister like Jessica, and a mother like Mrs Haggerthwaite, he seldom got one. Jessica always had some scheme or other, while Mrs Haggerthwaite – Mrs Haggerthwaite was a professional witch. It was true that the sort of

witchcraft Mrs Haggerthwaite went in for was more about selling people good luck charms for their driving tests, or boiling up anti-wart potions over a fire in the back garden, than flying around on a broomstick or battling with vampires or raising the dead. But having any kind of witch for a mother, in a small town like Bellstone, is bound to make life rather more exciting than one might like.

'I need a new challenge,' Jessica announced, further undermining Midge's sense of security. 'I was reading this book from the library – *How To Get What You Want From Life In Three Easy Stages.*

What you do is, you work out your Aim and write it down – that's Stage One – then you make out a list of how to get it – that's Stage Two – then you go out and follow the list. Stage Three. See! Easy-peasy!'

'Great,' said Midge, sarcastically. 'So why don't you write down *Aim: Take over the World*?'

'But I don't want to take over the world. I just want something exciting to happen.'

Jessica sighed. She did not know how to explain to Midge her sudden restlessness. Midge was quite happy with his everyday life: going to school, helping his dad with his landscape gardening business, playing football in the park or going to the school Art Club. But Jessica wanted something to happen. She wanted to do something big and important. The only trouble was, she did not know what.

'Everything's fine as it is,' Midge said crossly. 'I mean, what do you want? Bank robberies? Fire-breathing dragons? *People standing on their heads?*'

His voice had changed suddenly, but Jessica did not notice. Nor did she notice that Midge was now staring through the railings into Bellstone Public Park with his mouth wide open.

'Well, it would make things more interesting,' she said. 'But, of course, nobody would. Stand on their head, I mean. I expect most people in Bellstone would rather die than do something like that—'

She stopped with a squeak, because Midge had just grabbed her arm. He pointed into the park. 'So, what are those?' he demanded. 'Some new kind of flower they're growing?'

Jessica stared. For a moment all she could see beyond the railings were several large shrubs. But then she spotted two pink somethings emerging from the leaves. At first sight, they looked like large, exotic flowers. But then she realised the pink petals were not petals but *toes* – toes which belonged to feet. Rather pretty feet with glittering pink toenails – but definitely feet.

As she looked more closely, she saw a holly bush sprouting two black boots amongst its berries; while two slender legs waved from a willow tree, like additional branches.

Jessica's eyes gleamed. 'Something funny's going on! Let's investigate!'

They ran until they reached the gate into the park, then along a gravel path. They had almost reached the right spot when they saw a procession of people coming towards them, chanting, and waving their hands above their heads.

Jessica's eyes were immediately fixed on the tall woman leading the procession. This, Jessica saw,

was not the kind of person you usually met in Bellstone. She was more the kind of person you saw in films on TV. She was extremely pretty – beautiful, even – and very glamorous, with long, wavy blonde hair and a floaty pink tunic. She was also barefoot – and her toenails were pink and glittering.

The people following her were perfectly ordinary looking, except that they were all singing. Midge (who was less impressed with their leader than Jessica) tried to work out *what* they were singing, but all he could make out was a refrain: *The Spirits, The Spirits, Tra-la, Tra-la!*

Neither of them had any doubt that these were the same people who had been doing the headstands. They had spotted the black boots and pink toenails immediately.

'What's going on?' whispered Midge.

'I don't know,' Jessica said. But if there was one thing she hated (possibly even more than being bored) it was not knowing things. She waited until the procession had drawn level, then she stepped out in front of them.

'Hey,' she demanded. 'What's going on?'

The leader of the procession stopped – she didn't have much choice. But, even though she was right under her nose, the woman hardly seemed to notice Jessica was there. Jessica felt like a small, insignificant insect – and it was a most uncomfortable feeling.

'Little girl,' she murmured at last (so at least she had realised Jessica was not a ladybird or a beetle). 'Do you seek to impede our communion with the Spirits?'

Jessica had no idea what she meant, except that she had called her 'little girl', which was another of the things that Jessica particularly disliked. 'Who are you?' she asked.

'I am Xandra, Friend of the Wind Spirits,' murmured the woman, waving a crystal that was hanging from her neck. 'Do not interrupt our sacred march!'

'Why not?' Jessica asked. 'Anyway, I want to know what you're doing!'

Something changed in Xandra's face – like a lightbulb switching on. 'I daresay you do, dear,' she said, and she sounded quite sympathetic. 'But I'm afraid you couldn't afford my rates. But do give this to your parents. They can call me any time.' She fished something out of her pocket and pressed it into Jessica's hand. Then she set off again, her procession following her.

'Well! Did you ever see the like!' Jessica watched

for a moment, then she gave a squeak of surprise. She had spotted a girl of her own age. 'Hey! Who are you? What are you doing?'

The girl stopped short. Like Xandra, she had long blonde hair with a blue flower in it, and was also dressed in a tunic. Jessica, who would never have dreamt of putting flowers in her hair, did not take to her. And from the expression on *her* face, it was clear that the girl did not take to Jessica either. She was eyeing Jessica's windswept brown hair, workaday clothes and battered school bag in a very disdainful way.

'I am Agapanthus, Friend of the Wind Spirits,' she announced.

'Wow. What a horrible name,' said Midge, with sympathy.

Agapanthus scowled at him. 'It is not horrible! An Agapanthus is a beautiful blue flower!'

'We know that. Our dad's a gardener,' Jessica said. 'But if he'd called me that I'd have killed him!'

Agapanthus tossed her hair. 'The Spirits came to my mother in a dream and told her my name.'

Midge was even more sympathetic. 'Couldn't your dad stop her?'

'He wasn't very pleased about it,' Agapanthus admitted. 'But that doesn't matter. He doesn't live with us any more.'

'So, is that woman your mum?' asked Jessica, wanting to get things absolutely straight. 'Xandra Whatsits?'

Agapanthus nodded. Jessica and Midge looked at each other. Despite her haughty manner, both of them felt a rush of sympathy for this girl. Mothers who did strange things were something they understood. Both were agreeing silently on no account to say, 'she must be crazy,' or 'who does she think she is?' They had both suffered enough from people saying exactly these things about their *own* mother.

Instead, Jessica said, quite kindly, 'I'm surprised we haven't heard of her. I mean there aren't many – err – Friends of the Wind Spirits in Bellstone.'

Agapanthus tossed her head. 'You haven't heard of her because we've only just arrived. But don't worry, you soon will. Mum's going to take this town by storm. There's nothing here at the moment, she says, in her line – just some mouldy old woman who thinks she's a witch! And she's no threat at all!' And with this remark she took off, the gravel flying beneath her heels.

'Well!' Jessica gasped. Then she recovered herself and yelled, 'That's what you think!' after the vanishing Agapanthus. Then she turned to Midge. 'She was talking about Mum!'

'I know. Let's have a look at that.'

Jessica had forgotten the thing that Xandra had handed her. It turned out to be a leaflet, with a picture of Xandra on the front. Inside, it said: 'Fly With the Spirits! Find Inner Truth! Achieve Perfect Physical Health! Consult Xandra, Friend of the Wind Spirits, Mystic to the Stars!' In smaller type was a telephone number and, 'Hourly rates available on request'.

'What *is* a Wind Spirit?' asked Midge.

'I don't know,' said Jessica. But she was thinking. And the more she thought about Xandra and her strange procession, the more it reminded her of the

kind of things Mrs Haggerthwaite got up to. Of course, Mrs Haggerthwaite would not have dreamt of standing on her head in the park (although she had once danced in her underwear on the roof of the Haggerthwaites' house); nor did she wear floaty tunics and crystals (although some of the things she did wear were just as odd). But processing around the place, chanting strange, incomprehensible chants – that was exactly the kind of thing she *did* do.

It seemed to Jessica that Xandra, Friend of the Wind Spirits, if not exactly a witch, must be something similar. Furthermore, she seemed to be looking for customers. Jessica had a feeling that her mother was not going to like this.

Quickly, Jessica explained it all to Midge. 'Just wait until Mum hears!' she finished. 'She'll hit the roof! You heard what that girl said – *there's only that mouldy old witch!* This Xandra is planning to take all Mum's customers!'

'You don't know that,' said Midge.

'It's obvious! Come on, let's go and tell Mum!' She turned to run, but Midge grabbed her by the back of her jumper. Jessica turned and found, to her astonishment, that Midge was glaring at her. His eyes were blazing, and his skin had gone so white that his freckles stood out like ink spots. Midge hardly ever lost his temper, but he looked close to it now.

'You never learn, do you?'

'How d'you mean?'

'What do you want to go charging in for, stirring up trouble! You never leave things alone.'

'But—'

'Look what happened last time you went rushing in! When Mum first went professional. I'll tell you what happened. Mum and Dad fighting – Mum getting in the papers – trouble at school – and Dad moving out.'

He paused for breath. Jessica stared at him in astonishment.

Of course, it was true enough. When Mrs Haggerthwaite had set up her own business as a professional witch – and Jessica had pledged to stop her – it had been a very difficult time for the Haggerthwaites. The worst point was when Mr Haggerthwaite had moved out and gone to stay with his sister, Jessica and Midge's Aunt Kate. Midge especially had been really miserable. Still, Jessica could not help thinking he was overreacting. All that was in the past now. It had nothing to do with Xandra, Friend of the Wind Spirits.

'But I don't mean—' Jessica began.

'You never *do* mean things. But they happen.

Once you start stirring things up they do, anyway.' Midge took a deep breath. 'I don't *want* any excitement,' he declared passionately. 'I've had enough to last me a lifetime!'

Jessica opened her mouth to tell him how silly he was being. Then, much to her surprise, she shut it again. She still could not see why he was so upset. But something in his anguished expression made her feel that she should pay attention.

'All right,' she said. 'I promise I won't say anything to Mum, not if you don't want me to.'

'Good.'

'Although she's bound to find out, sooner or later.'

A look of sudden fear passed across Midge's face. He said quickly, 'I don't care! Maybe she won't find out. Anyway, I don't want you to tell her.'

'All right!' For a few minutes they walked on in silence. Midge was relieved, but Jessica felt frustrated and restless. Life, which had looked like it might be going to get more lively, had reverted to boredom again.

'Still, at least you can't say nothing exciting ever happens,' said Midge at last, in a more normal voice.

'Huh. Call that exciting! They were just standing on their heads, under the trees. Not flying out of them – now *that* would have been exciting.' She snorted, thinking that nothing was less likely. 'I need a challenge! I want to be famous!' she burst out suddenly. Then she shrugged. 'Oh, come on. I'll race you to the gate!'

But as it turned out, their plans counted for nothing. As they reached their front door, it flew open and Mrs Haggerthwaite shot out, in a swirl of black hair and cloak. With an 'Ooof!' she ran straight into Jessica and the two of them went hurtling across the path, just avoiding Midge, and

ending up in the middle of a large and prickly rose bush.

'Mum!' yelled Jessica, when she had extracted herself from the bush. 'What d'you think you're doing?'

'*Me?* What do you think *you're* doing, lurking around where people can run into you?' demanded Mrs Haggerthwaite unreasonably – in fact, so unreasonably that Jessica could think of nothing to say. Mrs Haggerthwaite was very good at taking the wind out of people's sails in this way.

Mrs Haggerthwaite was very tall, with green eyes, a big nose and long black hair. In fact, she looked the way a witch is supposed to look. Neither of her children (much to their relief) looked much like her. Midge had sandy hair and freckles, like his dad, and Jessica had brown eyes and curls, like her Aunt Kate.

'You should be more careful, Mum,' said Midge. 'You might have squashed Liverwort.' He patted the toad, who was trembling.

'Oh, there's no danger of that,' said Mrs Haggerthwaite, picking thorns from her dress. 'He is my familiar, and I can sense his presence from his cosmic rays.'

'Huh,' said Jessica. 'I notice you didn't sense *my* presence from *my* cosmic rays.'

'That's different,' said Mrs Haggerthwaite. 'Anyway, that's not important. I was coming to look for you. I have news. News of some import.' She looked from face to face. 'I have just heard – just this moment – that a fellow traveller is arrived in Bellstone. I mean by that – another *magical practitioner.*'

Her children stared at her blankly for a moment. Then Jessica said, 'What – you mean another witch?'

'That's right. One of my clients, Mrs Culver, told me, while I was mixing up a new potion for her athlete's foot. Although it sounds like she might be more *mystical* than *magical*, if you know what I mean.'

'Umm – I think we might,' said Jessica. 'Mum. Do you mean you're actually pleased about this, err, new arrival?'

'Of course I am! I've always hoped one day another witch would move to Bellstone. Somebody who understands what it's like. Someone to share the burdens and joys of witchcraft!'

'Oh.' Jessica did not know what else to say.

'I'm going to visit her,' Mrs Haggerthwaite continued. 'To welcome her to the neighbourhood. I shall take Liverwort. This new witch may have a familiar he would like to meet.' Another thought struck her. 'And I must take a present. I know – a bottle of my sow thistle unguent. You can never have too much sow thistle unguent!'

She disappeared into the house. Midge and Jessica stared at each other.

'Does she mean Xandra Wind Spirit?' Midge whispered.

'I think she must,' said Jessica. 'And she doesn't mind after all.' Secretly, she felt disappointed, although she could see that Midge was relieved. But she still felt curious about Xandra. 'I'll go too,' Jessica decided.

In a moment, Mrs Haggerthwaite was back. Midge said he would go and meet his father and come home with him, so Mrs Haggerthwaite and Jessica set out on their own.

Chapter Two

Mrs Haggerthwaite was not sure which house the new witch lived in; she only knew that she lived on Lavender Gardens. 'But my magical powers will soon detect the presence of a Sister in Witchcraft and lead me to her,' she told Jessica. Personally, Jessica was not convinced by this and wondered if she should fetch out her leaflet and look for an address. But as it turned out neither Mrs Haggerthwaite's magical powers nor Jessica's leaflet were required. For as they drew near number seven Lavender Gardens, they spotted a large sign in the garden. It showed a photo of Xandra, dressed in her pink tunic, and apparently flying through the air with her arms outstretched. Above the photo was written in gold letters:

XANDRA, FRIEND OF THE WIND SPIRITS!

Mrs Haggerthwaite regarded the sign in silence, for a long time.

'Humph,' she said at last. 'I'm sure a poster of that size breaks all the local planning laws.'

Jessica thought this a bit rich, given that Mrs Haggerthwaite herself never took any notice of rules and regulations. She always claimed that witches were above that kind of thing. But before she could point this out Mrs Haggerthwaite went on, 'And what a name! Xandra – I don't even know how you pronounce it.'

'Xandra,' murmured a voice just behind her. It gave the 'X' sound a sibilant hiss, like a snake. '*Xxxxxandra*. That's how you pronounce it.'

Mrs Haggerthwaite jumped. Her magical powers of detection had obviously failed her on this occasion, for this was certainly Xandra, Friend of the Wind Spirits, and Mrs Haggerthwaite had not detected her.

'Do you always creep up like that?' she said crossly.

'Only when the Spirits summon me,' said Xandra mysteriously. She looked the same as in the park, except she now had a pink scarf tied around her head. 'Come,' she murmured. 'Follow me, into the Sanctum of the Spirits!' And she set off with a gliding motion.

'Huh,' said Mrs Haggerthwaite. 'Sanctum of the Spirits, indeed!' Somehow, Mrs Haggerthwaite no longer seemed quite so keen to meet her Sister in Witchcraft. In fact, she sounded positively grumpy.

'We may as well go and see,' suggested Jessica, who was curious.

They followed Xandra round the side of the house and into a garden which was so overgrown that for a moment they lost sight of Xandra herself. Then they spotted her, sitting under a tree, with her legs twisted in front of her. Jessica stared. She was pretty sure that her mother could not sit with her legs wound round each other like that. In the branches above, wind chimes clinked gently.

'Approach,' murmured Xandra. 'Approach and tell the Spirits what you seek.' In a completely different tone of voice, she added, 'Payment by the hour, but I'll let the kid come free,' and she whipped out a piece of paper from her sleeve and handed it to Mrs Haggerthwaite.

'But this is twice as much as I charge!' declared Mrs Haggerthwaite, inspecting the list of prices. 'Besides, I'm not a customer.'

'Aren't you?' Xandra sounded disappointed. 'I was sure you must be. I gave your little girl my leaflet in the park.' And while Mrs Haggerthwaite looked at Jessica in surprise, Xandra unwound her legs and sat back against the tree trunk in a more normal manner. 'What *do* you want, then?'

'Mum's here to welcome you to Bellstone,' Jessica explained. 'You see, she's in a similar line to you. She's a witch.'

'Ah! So you're Bellstone's famous witch.'

Mrs Haggerthwaite could not help smiling. 'Yes, I suppose I *am* quite well known,' she said, looking rather smug.

'But how terribly old fashioned!'

Mrs Haggerthwaite stopped smiling. 'Old fashioned?' she said in a dangerous voice. 'What d'you mean, *old fashioned*?'

'Well, really: *witches*.' Xandra gave a tinkly laugh. 'That sort of thing went out years ago. *Centuries*, I should think. It's so peasanty. So medieval. All those warty old women putting spells on people and being thrown into duck ponds. Such smelly old spells with such unpleasant ingredients! Eye of newt and all that. No, things have moved on since then.'

Mrs Haggerthwaite looked as if she was going to explode. Before she could do so, Jessica said quickly, 'But what are you, Mrs – umm – Wind Spirit, if you're not a witch?'

'Do call me Xandra. And why don't the two of you sit down?' She gestured at the grass in front of her.

Mrs Haggerthwaite looked as if Xandra had offered her the compost heap. 'I'd rather not,' she snapped. 'It looks damp to me. And if we are going to discuss this, I would rather it was indoors, over a cup of tea.'

Xandra sighed. 'I'd much prefer to stay here. I find the Spirits speak so much more clearly through trees and flowers. Still, I suppose you witches wouldn't understand that. I suppose dark, smoky kitchens are the kind of places you witches like.'

And in one quick, fluid movement she had risen from the ground and was heading back to the house. It was lucky for her that she *was* so quick and fluid. Otherwise, Mrs Haggerthwaite might well have kicked her. She was scarlet with rage. 'Who does she think she is?' she demanded of Jessica. 'Just because I don't want to sit around in the mud! And there's nothing dark and smoky about *my* kitchen – whatever hers may be like!'

'I expect,' said Jessica wisely, 'she just doesn't know much about witches. After all, a lot of people *do* expect witches to live in dark, spooky places – and to be wicked, of course.'

Mrs Haggerthwaite had to admit that was true – much to Jessica's relief, for she was terribly curious to find out more about Xandra. Until now, Jessica had always thought there were two kinds of people in the world. First there were sensible, down-to-earth people, like Mr Haggerthwaite and Aunt Kate and Jessica herself. They didn't believe in magic and wanted nothing to do with 'all that twaddle', as Aunt Kate called it. These people were usually interested in sensible, practical things, like gardening (Mr Haggerthwaite) or cooking (Aunt Kate) or, best of all, science (like Jessica herself). Science, Jessica sometimes thought dreamily, was so very exact, and careful, and precise (whereas witchcraft was vague and full of gobbledegook) – and yet sometimes science blossomed unexpectedly into a kind of magic of its own. One day, Jessica meant to do science all the time – and be world famous too.

In the meantime, however, she often had to deal with people like her mother, who were not sensible at all. They talked about 'Other Planes of Being' and 'Tapping into the Cosmic Dimension' and went in for spells and charms and gazing into crystal balls. In Jessica's experience these people were either witches, like Mrs Haggerthwaite and her friends, or people who believed in witchcraft, like Mrs Haggerthwaite's customers. And now here was this new person, who sounded almost as mad as Mrs Haggerthwaite herself, and yet who was not a witch. Perhaps it was her inquiring scientific mind, but Jessica was suddenly determined to find out all about her.

They followed Xandra into the kitchen, which was not dark or smoky in the slightest. There were wind chimes and a row of crystals on the windowsill, but other than that it was no stranger than the Haggerthwaites' own. And it was probably cleaner.

Xandra did not say anything else rude, but instead became extremely friendly, sitting them down and plying them with tea and biscuits. Xandra explained that the tea was made of geraniums, because geranium was her 'Spirit Flower', and although Jessica thought it tasted rather strange, it was no worse than Mrs Haggerthwaite's own nettle brew. The tea seemed to restore Mrs Haggerthwaite's good humour, and when Jessica reminded her, she even produced her gift of sow thistle unguent. Admittedly, Xandra did not look terribly thrilled to receive it, even when Mrs Haggerthwaite (glancing at Xandra's bare feet) explained that as well as promoting youthful skin it could help prevent verrucas.

'Now, why don't you tell me all about your witchcraft?' Xandra murmured to Mrs Haggerthwaite, her voice as sweet as honey.

Mrs Haggerthwaite was only too happy to oblige. And in no time at all she was deep in the story of how she became Bellstone's one and only professional witch.

'I'd been a practising witch for years. Of course, I'm not the type you read about in storybooks. I don't go flying about on a broomstick or turn people into frogs. No, I'm interested in the old ways – spells and potions that have been passed down from generation to generation, forgotten ways with herbs, old charms that heal or protect. It took a while to build up business. But now I'm doing very well. You'll find I have quite a following in Bellstone.' She smiled smugly. She looked just like Liverwort did, after he had eaten a particularly large and juicy slug.

'How quaint,' said Xandra.

Mrs Haggerthwaite looked as if the slug was not so tasty after all.

Jessica saw that she would have to intervene quickly, if she was to find out anything more about Xandra before her mother stormed out.

'So, what are you,' Jessica asked, 'if you're not a witch?'

Xandra gazed into the air above Jessica's left ear. 'I am one who floats on the Winds . . . I am one who speaks with the Spirits.'

'Is that what you put on your passport?' asked Jessica, genuinely curious.

'Or your tax return,' said Mrs Haggerthwaite snippily.

Jessica said, 'But what *is* a Wind Spirit?'

'A Wind Spirit is what it says – a Spirit of the Wind.'

'Are you sure you don't mean *full* of wind?' asked Mrs Haggerthwaite nastily. 'Because if so, I have a potion I could give you. It will make you burp less – and, err, other things as well. Several of my clients swear by it. Of course, maybe you just mean you're full of hot air – I'm afraid there's not much I can do about that. Except to try and bring you down to earth.'

Jessica asked quickly, 'But what exactly do you believe in? And what exactly do you do?'

Xandra was beginning to look less vague and dreamy, and more annoyed and irritated. 'My poor child!' she said now. 'Always wanting an explanation!'

'I'm going to be a scientist,' said Jessica promptly. 'So of course I want explanations.'

Xandra sighed. 'What a shame! Still, I expect you are simply reacting against your upbringing. It's

hardly surprising. With a mother stuck in the Dark Ages!'

This did not please either of her listeners. Jessica was furious to have her scientific ambitions spoken of in this way (and especially by the suggestion that she was only trying to be different from her mother) while Mrs Haggerthwaite did not take kindly to being described as 'stuck in the Dark Ages'.

'We witches are extremely modern, I'll have you know,' she declared. 'In fact we are bang up to date!'

'Oh really?' Xandra murmured. 'Do you have a website, I wonder?'

'Err – well – not exactly.'

Xandra tutted. 'That's very foolish. Nobody gets anywhere in business without one. Not in our line.'

'That's where you're wrong,' Mrs Haggerthwaite retorted. 'I've already told you, I run my own business, and it's doing very well!'

'You may have been doing all right – so far. After all, you've had Bellstone pretty much to yourself. There wasn't any real competition. But now there is.' Xandra smiled sweetly and pushed a plate towards them. 'Do have another biscuit, won't you? No, we'll see how your business is doing a month from now. We'll see how many customers you have left.'

Despite the sugar in her voice, it sounded very like a threat.

Jessica had to run to keep up with her mother, who was charging along the street like an enraged hippo. Jessica was in a bad mood herself especially as, just as they were leaving, Agapanthus had suddenly appeared and, staring at Jessica, demanded, 'What's *she* doing here?' in a sneering and disdainful voice. Jessica was thinking so hard about how much she disliked Agapanthus that she did not notice when Mrs Haggerthwaite stopped short, and she went cannoning into the back of her.

'Do pay attention, Jessica!' snapped Mrs Haggerthwaite, continuing at once, 'That Xandra! Just who does she think she is? Witchcraft has been around for hundreds of years, and she comes along, a puny little upstart like her, and claims to be able to do things better. She's almost as bad as you scientists!'

'She's nothing like us scientists!' declared Jessica indignantly.

'And where's the evidence for her fiddle-faddle? That's what I want to know!'

Jessica found this funny. 'Well, there isn't much evidence for witchcraft, either,' she pointed out.

'Of course there is!'

'Like what?'

'Don't quibble,' Mrs Haggerthwaite snapped. 'And don't try to sidetrack me, either. The point is that woman is hoodwinking the public! And she shouldn't be allowed to get away with it. Listen to this,' and Mrs Haggerthwaite began reading from the leaflet that Xandra Wind Spirit had given her. '*Look into the future . . . overcome health problems . . . enjoy prosperity*— Prosperity! At the prices she's charging!'

'Well, you claim to do those things too,' Jessica pointed out.

'That's different!'

'Yes. You make people drink nasty potions. She makes them stand on their heads.'

'As if standing on your head would do anything other than make you look extremely silly,' said Mrs Haggerthwaite icily. Jessica giggled. Obviously prancing about the garden in your underwear while chanting incantations, or gathering mistletoe from the apple tree by the light of a full moon (both things that Mrs Haggerthwaite had been known to do), did not look silly at all. Her mother turned on her.

'And another thing. Why haven't I got a website? I'm disappointed in you, Jessica.'

'What do you mean?'

'Well, you're the scientist. You know about

computers and things. It's the least you could do.'

Jessica was so angry she could hardly speak. 'How can I make you a website,' she managed to get out at last, 'when I don't even have a computer!'

Her eyes sparkled with anger. The truth was, as Mrs Haggerthwaite well knew, that Jessica longed for a computer. In particular, she longed to get on the Internet, so that she could find out all kinds of scientific information, and download pictures of galaxies and the like.

But she did not have one – and that was down to Mrs Haggerthwaite.

'We witches just don't get along with them,' Mrs Haggerthwaite would declare, whenever Jessica raised the matter. 'They give out cosmic rays, you know. And those wreak havoc with my witchcraft.'

Jessica and Mr Haggerthwaite would tell her that this was absolute rubbish, but there was no persuading her. Jessica would read out pages from her *Junior Science Encyclopaedia* but Mrs Haggerthwaite would not listen. Mr Haggerthwaite had tried another approach.

'But there are computers everywhere!' he would declare. 'In banks! Supermarkets! Libraries!'

'I know,' replied Mrs Haggerthwaite stubbornly. 'Every time I go into one of those places I can feel them sapping my magical energy.'

Mr Haggerthwaite had given up, worried that his wife would start refusing to visit banks and libraries and supermarkets too. But it was no wonder that Jessica was filled with outrage now.

Mrs Haggerthwaite, however, did not back down easily.

'I don't see why it matters whether you have a computer. If scientists can understand the stars without travelling in starships, then I don't see why you actually *need* a computer to make me a website.'

'But Mum! It's completely different.'

'Anyway,' said Mrs Haggerthwaite, striding on

again, 'that's not important now. What *is* important is what I'm going to do about this Xandra, Friend of the Whatsits!'

'What do you mean?'

'I mean, something must be done! I've a good mind to report her to the Council! Or throw whitewash over that sign of hers. Or maybe I'll stand outside her house with a placard – *Wind Spirits Keep Out.*'

Jessica's thoughts were spinning. A campaign like this would certainly make life more exciting! She imagined herself giving interviews to the media, as

Mrs Haggerthwaite was led away from Lavender Gardens in handcuffs. 'Eleven-year-old Jessica Haggerthwaite, already acknowledged as a budding

scientific genius, spoke today about what it is like having a mother who's a witch—' But then she remembered her conversation with Midge, and how much he hated fuss. And the kind of things Mrs Haggerthwaite was suggesting sounded like fuss on a major scale. With a pang of regret, Jessica said, 'Don't you think you're overreacting?'

'Overreacting! To somebody like that, who's going to steal my customers, and cheat them out of every penny! Who calls us witches quaint and old fashioned! No, the more I think about it, the angrier I get!' Mrs Haggerthwaite stood still for a moment, her eyes flashing fire, as she contemplated the general awfulness of Xandra, while Jessica searched desperately for some way to calm her down. 'No, she's so dreadful, there's only one thing for it!'

'What's that?' asked Jessica nervously.

'I thought at first it was going too far, but now I see that she deserves it. I shall curse her! Not an evil, wicked curse, of course. I don't touch those. But I shall do an Incantation – an Incantation to Open the Eyes of Bellstone to her Deceptions!'

'Oh, right,' said Jessica, relieved. 'Yes, that's a good idea. And you'll forget about the whitewash and the placard?'

'They hardly signify now,' said Mrs

Haggerthwaite grandly. She walked on a way, then added, 'Although there is one problem. Your father. He doesn't like me cursing people. Even if it's just a mild one. And I want to get started right away.'

Jessica did not want Mrs Haggerthwaite to change her mind. An Incantation was infinitely better (being much less likely to get her arrested) than any of her other ideas. Jessica thought hard, then said quickly, 'I'll tell you what. Me and Midge will go and meet Dad after school tomorrow, and delay him. Then you can do your Incantation in peace, after your clients have left.' Mrs Haggerthwaite agreed to this, and Jessica added, 'But there is one condition. You mustn't let Midge know. I don't know why, but he hates the idea of you and Xandra fighting.'

Mrs Haggerthwaite nodded. Now she had a chance to think more calmly, she knew that Mr Haggerthwaite would disapprove of her feuding with Xandra, and she could see that it would be better if he and Midge knew as little as possible.

They spent the rest of their walk home in happy discussion about how silly Xandra had looked in her pink tunic.

When they opened the front door a gorgeous smell greeted them. Mr Haggerthwaite and Midge were back, and Mr Haggerthwaite was cooking. In what seemed no time at all, they were sitting down and Mr Haggerthwaite was passing round the piping hot food.

'Now,' he said, doling out potatoes. 'Where have you been? Midge was saying something about there being a new witch in Bellstone, and that you'd gone to meet her.'

'Never mind that,' said Jessica quickly. She could see her mother turning red in the face at the very thought of Xandra, and she had a feeling that, in the heat of the moment, Mrs Haggerthwaite might forget their agreement. 'What have you been doing today, Dad?'

'I've been down at the hotel,' her father replied. 'I've drawn up some designs, and I'm sure Bert Flotsam's going to like them. It's going to look a treat.'

His eyes glowed as he described his ideas. He had been a gardener for years, but had only recently set up his own business. Bert Flotsam was the father of one of Jessica's friends and he owned the biggest hotel in Bellstone. Mr Haggerthwaite was landscaping the gardens there – it was his first big job.

His enthusiasm was infectious. It seemed quite natural for Jessica to ask, 'Can me and Midge come over tomorrow and see?'

'I was there today,' said Midge. 'But I'd like to go again. I might do some drawings for Art Club.'

Mr Haggerthwaite agreed at once. Then he remembered his earlier question and turned to his wife. 'But Mel, what's all this about another witch in town?'

'Witch!' exclaimed Mrs Haggerthwaite indignantly – so indignantly that a piece of carrot went down the wrong way and she began to choke. Mr Haggerthwaite got up and banged his wife on the back. Jessica gave her mother a nudge. 'Err – well, she's not exactly a witch,' said Mrs Haggerthwaite.

'No? What is she then? There's not a problem is there?' asked Mr Haggerthwaite. He sounded anxious. Midge had laid down his fork and was looking worried too. 'You haven't fallen out with her, have you?'

Mrs Haggerthwaite caught Jessica's eye. 'No – certainly not. As you know, I'm always interested to meet new people. Even if this – err, Xandra, as she calls herself – even if she isn't a witch in the usual sense. Actually, I'm not sure what she is.' And she put a potato in her mouth, to stop herself from saying anything more.

Mr Haggerthwaite looked reassured. 'It'll be nice for you, having a like-minded person in the neighbourhood. Maybe you'll be friends. I know I always enjoy it when I can have a good chat with another gardener.'

'Hmm,' said Mrs Haggerthwaite darkly. Jessica gave her a sharp kick under the table. 'Owww! Err, yes, Xandra and me, I expect we shall be best of friends in no time,' she went on in a falsely hearty manner. 'Now, Tom, tell me more about your ideas for the hotel gardens.'

Later that evening, Jessica sat on her bed with her geography homework propped up against her knees. But she was not thinking about geography. She was brooding again on the vexed issue of *Life*, and *How to Make it More Exciting*.

She glanced round at all her things. There were her pine desk and bookcase that Mrs Haggerthwaite had found in a junk shop, and Mr Haggerthwaite and Jessica had sanded and varnished until they were good as new. There was the clay model of Liverwort that Midge had made her at Art Club. There was the article about Jessica which had appeared in the *Bellstone Gazette*, and which was now hanging on the wall in a special frame Mr Haggerthwaite had made. There was her stuffed owl, Twoo, sitting on her bedside table. Best of all, there were her science things: her microscope, her *Junior Science Encyclopaedia*, her collection of fossils, and her posters of dinosaurs and the Solar System and Marie Curie.

It was all very familiar. At this moment, perhaps *too* familiar.

Her thoughts were broken by a thump at the door. The next moment Mrs Haggerthwaite staggered in, carrying a heavy, black object. She lurched across the room and set it down with a bang on Jessica's desk.

'Watch out!' Jessica yelped. 'You almost knocked over my microscope!'

'There,' said Mrs Haggerthwaite triumphantly. 'You said you wanted a computer!'

Jessica stared at the object on her desk. Then she stared at her mother. Of course, she had always known that Mrs Haggerthwaite was a bit out of touch when it came to anything that wasn't witchcraft – especially anything technological. All the same, she hadn't thought she was *this* out of touch.

'Mum, that is not a computer! That is a typewriter.' She looked more closely and added, 'A very old, dusty typewriter.'

'Yes, I'd forgotten we had one in the loft. Well, it's the same kind of thing as a computer isn't it?' said Mrs Haggerthwaite airily.

'It's not the same kind of thing at all!'

'They both have keyboards, don't they?'

'So do pianos!'

'This just doesn't have all those wires that computers have. Which is a good thing, because it's the wires that give off those cosmic rays, you know—'

'I know,' interrupted Jessica heavily. 'The ones that sap your magical energy.'

'That's right,' said Mrs Haggerthwaite. 'Well, have fun.' And she disappeared. Jessica ran onto the landing after her.

'I'll do some programming shall I?' she shouted. 'Or surf the web?' But Mrs Haggerthwaite just smiled and waved.

Back in her room, Jessica inspected the typewriter again. It was old and dusty, but it didn't look like there was anything else wrong with it. She found a piece of blank paper and fed it into the machine.

```
AIM: Make Life More Exciting
(1)
```

The keys jammed and Jessica's thoughts jammed with them. She was just unjamming the keys (and getting ink all over her hands) when there was a thump at the door and Midge came in.

'Oh, it's you,' said Jessica. 'What do you want? And can I borrow some paper?'

'You can have some of my art paper if you buy me some more,' said Midge. He fetched the paper, then sat down on Jessica's bed, balancing Liverwort on one knee. 'I've been thinking. Why don't you go on television?'

'Are you trying to be funny?' Jessica's head poked out over the machine.

'You wanted to make life more exciting.'

'I know, but—'

'Well, you've already been in the *Bellstone Gazette*, talking about science. So why not TV?'

Jessica stared at him.

'Then you'd be an all-round media star!'

'Hmm,' said Jessica. She was remembering her earlier vision of herself, giving interviews about Mrs Haggerthwaite to the papers. Better still to be on TV! And better yet if it had nothing to do with Mrs Haggerthwaite. 'Of course, not nearly enough TV is given over to serious science topics,' she said at last. 'Especially not kids' TV. They think all kids are only interested in pop groups, pets and cartoons. They don't realise that there are far more interesting subjects. Like nuclear fission!'

'Err, yes,' said Midge. He was thinking about the kids he knew in Bellstone. Apart from Jessica, he could not think of a single one likely to be interested in nuclear fission. On the other hand, he knew quite a few people who were interested in pop groups, pets and cartoons. Something told him it would not be wise to point this out.

'So,' he said, 'why don't you write and say you'll be happy to do a programme on – err – nuclear whatsits.'

'Why not?' said Jessica, her eyes gleaming. 'I'll tell them there's a gap in the market. I'll send in a copy of my article from the *Gazette* too, so they'll realise I'm to be taken seriously.'

Midge grinned and got up to go.

'You know something,' said Jessica warmly. 'Sometimes you really do have good ideas!'

Midge thought so too. Ever since their conversation that afternoon, he had been trying to think of a suitable challenge to keep her out of trouble. Something difficult, to take up her time and energy, and prevent her making trouble for everyone else. As he went back to his own room, he thought he might just have managed it.

Half an hour later, Jessica had typed out a list.

AIM: To Become TV Star
    (1) Write letter to TV company

(2) Post letter to TV company
(3) Get Mum to buy me a new outfit. Something glamorous!

Then she got going on the letter. After a few false attempts (it was unfortunate, thought Jessica, that typewriters, unlike computers, would not correct your spelling for you) she had finished.

Dear TV Producer,

Have you thought that there are not enough programmes about science for children? Many children like science much more than cartoons and pop music. I should know, as I am eleven years old and I like science very much.

I would be happy to research and present some programmes on science for you. Here are a few of my ideas:

What is a Black Hole?
What if a Giant Asteroid Hits Earth?
Why Did the Dinosaurs Die Out?
How Do Bumble Bees Fly?
What is Nuclear Fission?

Please write and tell me what you

think. (I can think of plenty more topics if you don't like these ones.)

I enclose a recent article from the 'Bellstone Gazette', so you can see I am to be taken seriously.

Yours respectfully

Jessica Haggerthwaite (Ms)

Then she wrote in pencil (because her fingers were hurting after all that typing) on her original list: *It was a good idea of Midge's for me to become a TV star. Only how do I find out which address to write to? I am not sure they list TV companies in the Bellstone Telephone Directory, but I will look tomorrow.*

By this time it was quite late. As she got ready for bed, Jessica kept imagining herself on a TV screen. She could not decide whether she would wear a crisp white lab coat, to look as much as possible like a professional scientist, or a sharp little suit perhaps with a pair of horn-rimmed spectacles. Nevertheless, once curled up under the duvet, her final thoughts were about Xandra. She was still curious about her. But it was silly of Mrs Haggerthwaite to get so worked up about her, Jessica thought sleepily. Certainly, she was not worth the time and energy of somebody who was going to be a Media Star.

Chapter Three

Jessica had been deep in a dream in which she was interviewing Albert Einstein on TV, and did not hear her parents call her next morning.

She hurried to school with Midge, late, and feeling sad that however successful a TV star she became she would never be able to interview Albert Einstein (unless Xandra could arrange for her to interview him in spirit, she thought with a sudden snort). She slipped into her seat, hoping that her teacher, Miss Barnaby, would not spot her late arrival. Then she saw who was standing next to Miss Barnaby. It was a nasty shock.

'This,' Miss Barnaby said, 'is a new member of the class – Agapanthus. Welcome to West Bellstone Primary, dear.'

Jessica scowled. It was the same Agapanthus all right (it was hardly likely that there would be two girls with that name in Bellstone). The blonde hair was the same, and the tunic, and the snooty expression as she caught sight of Jessica was exactly the same too.

'I expect your friends call you Aggie, don't they?' asked Miss Barnaby kindly.

Agapanthus sniffed. 'They call me Agapanthus, *always*.'

'I see. I just thought—'

'Agapanthus is my Spirit Flower, you see.'

'Your Spirit Flower—'

'Yes, and it determines the colour of my aura, too. My aura is the most beautiful blue, just like an agapanthus flower.'

'Well, isn't that interesting,' Miss Barnaby gasped.

'Yes. It is. My mum says she will come in and tell the school all about auras and Wind Spirits, if you like. She might even do it for free.'

Agapanthus spoke as if she was offering a great favour. Miss Barnaby clearly did not know what to say but just stood there, opening and shutting her mouth like a goldfish.

'Well, that's kind of her,' she said at last. 'Now, Jessica will look after you. Her mother is a witch, you know. So you two should have a lot in common.'

It was hard to say which of Jessica and Agapanthus was less pleased. Jessica scowled, and Agapanthus sniffed. But there was nothing to be done.

At break-time, Jessica led her new charge into the playground. But before she could even begin a tour of the school, a crowd of girls came racing up and surrounded Agapanthus.

'Is your aura really blue?'

'What colour's my aura?'

'Do I have a Spirit Flower?'

'Does that crystal you're wearing bring you luck?'

Jessica found herself on the edge of the group, watching with a strange mixture of feelings. On the one hand, there was no danger that she was going to be landed with taking care of Agapanthus. There were plenty of people happy to do it for her. On the other, she was not sure how she felt about Agapanthus becoming (or so it seemed) the most popular girl in the school.

Clare, who was usually a good friend of Jessica's, caught her eye, and asked, 'So, is this the same type of stuff your mum does, spirits and auras and that?'

'No,' said Jessica, very firmly indeed.

Agapanthus said, 'Witchcraft has nothing to do with what *my* mother does.'

'Why's that?' asked Clare.

'Because witches are terribly old fashioned,' said Agapanthus. 'Quite out of date. Her mum did come to see my mum, actually. I think she wanted help with her spells. But my mother wasn't interested.'

'That's rubbish!' said Jessica indignantly. 'My mother doesn't need help! And she thinks your mother's stuff is silly!'

But nobody was listening. Jessica was put out. Usually her classmates were very interested in what she had to say.

She went and sat by herself near the railings and read through her letter to the TV company again.

'Hiya, Jessie!'

'Ouch!' Jessica recoiled from Robbie Flotsam, who had chosen to accompany his greeting by punching her playfully in the stomach. 'And don't call me Jessie!' But, despite the punch, he was grinning at her in a friendly way, and despite her crossness she was secretly pleased to see him. At least he was one person who was unlikely to be bowled over by crystals and Wind Spirits.

Robbie Flotsam was the toughest boy in the school and had become friends with Jessica, the smartest girl in the school, almost by accident. His father, Mr Flotsam, was the businessman who owned Bellstone's biggest hotel, where Mr Haggerthwaite was landscaping the gardens. Mr Flotsam also owned the *Bellstone Gazette*, which had published an article about Jessica.

'I've got something for you,' said Robbie. He held out a small, brown, mottled lump. It stared at Jessica out of reproachful brown eyes.

'Liverwort!'

'I rescued him from the rubbish skip. I had to nick the janitor's broom to get him out. Fell in myself, first,' he added cheerfully.

'That's why you've orange peel in your hair.' Jessica stroked Liverwort. 'This is Midge's fault! He shouldn't bring him to school.'

'Yeah, well, I don't think Liverwort minded. He was eating a dead goldfish.'

Jessica shuddered. 'It's lucky you found him. You know, I'm beginning to worry about Midge.'

Robbie shrugged. To his mind, there was nothing peculiar in taking a toad to school. 'Why are you over here by yourself?'

'I'm supposed to be looking after Agapanthus,' said Jessica. 'But I couldn't bear it. Agapanthus – what a name! And look at her hair! She looks like Goldilocks!'

'Her hair's quite pretty,' said Robbie. 'It *is* a stupid name though.'

'Her hair's not pretty at all! And her mum is trying to put *my* mum out of business.'

'Well, you've spent a lot of time trying to put your mum out of business,' Robbie pointed out.

'That's not the point!' Jessica glared at him.

Robbie decided to change the subject. He indicated the letter. 'What's that?'

Jessica hesitated. 'Promise you won't tell anyone?' He nodded. 'I'm planning to go on TV. Read this.'

Robbie finished reading and whistled through his teeth. 'It's hard to get on TV,' he observed.

'I know that!' Jessica was a bit disappointed. She had hoped he would say it was a fantastic letter, and sure to succeed.

'Yeah, my dad knows this TV producer. He's always trying to get him to do a programme about the hotel. For the publicity, you know. But this TV guy never will.'

'I'm not surprised,' said Jessica. 'But my science programmes will be much more interesting than your dad's hotel.' Then she had an idea. 'Can you get me his address? Then I could send my letter to him.'

Robbie nodded, and it was agreed that they would get the address from Mr Flotsam when Jessica and Midge went over to the hotel that afternoon. With that, the bell rang, and it was time to go in.

As they walked to the hotel, Jessica lost no time in telling Midge exactly what she thought of him for letting Liverwort escape. Midge, who was divided between massive relief that Liverwort was safe, and huge annoyance that Robbie and Jessica should be the ones to find him, soon grabbed Liverwort and ran off in front. Jessica looked after him, with a troubled expression.

'I don't know.' She shook her head. 'He never used to take Liverwort everywhere. He's acting like a little kid.'

'Ah well,' said Robbie wisely. 'Everybody does, sometimes.'

Jessica thought this sounded uncommonly sensible (even if it was Robbie Flotsam, not noted for his understanding of other people, who was saying it). So they talked about other things until they arrived at the hotel, where the first thing they saw was Mr Flotsam, climbing into his Jaguar car.

'Ah, Robbie! And young Jessica! And I just saw Midge. He went racing off before I could say a word. Now where are you all off to?'

'We're going to see Dad,' said Jessica.

'Ah, yes. Excellent work he's doing! He was showing me his new designs today and I'm really pleased with them. But I must be off.'

'Mr Flotsam,' said Jessica quickly. 'Have you really got a friend who works in television?'

'Of course I do! But look at the time. I've got a tremendously important meeting to go to.' He slammed the door and drove off before Jessica could say another word. She was fuming.

Still, as they walked on, past the tennis courts and into the gardens, she forgot her annoyance. She had never really explored the hotel grounds before. As they walked, past croquet lawns and sundials, the gardens grew wilder and wilder with stands of silver birch, drifts of meadow flowers, and squirrels and birds in the branches above.

'It's gorgeous here!' said Jessica. 'Why did you never tell me?'

Robbie shrugged. 'It's all right, I s'pose,' he said. 'I never thought about it.'

They found Mr Haggerthwaite at the furthest end of the gardens, by the lake. He had been clearing some weed, but had stopped to watch two moorhens, paddling through the shallows. 'Look!' he said, and they watched together, until Robbie yawned, and the moorhens moved away.

'So, what do you think?' Mr Haggerthwaite asked, gesturing around him.

'It's wonderful!' said Jessica.

'You wait till I'm finished!' And with his eyes glowing, he began to describe his plans, until Jessica and Robbie could almost see the roses

blossoming, the leaves sprouting, and the clematis and honeysuckle cascading down trees and walls.

'The only thing is, I like this bit just as it is,' said Jessica. She looked around her, at the waist-high grasses, the butterflies moving from flower to flower, and the willows bent low over the lake.

'I do too,' Mr Haggerthwaite admitted. 'There's something special about this place.'

'Look!' said Robbie.

'A hare!' said Mr Haggerthwaite. 'I haven't seen one since I was a boy.'

They watched as it disappeared into the bushes. Then there was a scuffling of leaves behind them. They turned round, expecting to see another wild animal – a deer or fox. Instead Midge appeared, looking grubby but cheerful.

'Dad!' he said. 'Liverwort almost got eaten by a duck! And I've been drawing kingfishers!'

'I expect there's all kinds of wildlife here,' said Mr Haggerthwaite.

Jessica looked at her father. 'Do you have to change it?' she asked. 'Can't you keep this bit the way it is?'

Mr Haggerthwaite sat down on an old treestump. He looked worried. 'The truth is,' he said, 'I like it this way too. But Bert Flotsam wants a proper garden, and he's hired me to make one. He'll want roses here – or herbaceous borders – or a proper mowed lawn – or something oriental, with bamboo. And if I say I don't need this bit, he'll dig it up and turn it into more tennis courts, or a swimming pool.'

'Yeah!' said Robbie. 'With a wave machine and flumes – fantastic!'

The Haggerthwaites looked at him with disapproval – even Jessica and Midge, who enjoyed flumes themselves. As for Mr Haggerthwaite – he looked as if he could not believe his ears. Robbie said quickly, 'Still, it would be a shame for the birds and that.'

And then Jessica had an idea.

'Make it a Wilderness Garden!'

'A Wilderness Garden?'

'Yes. Tell him it's *Scientifically Important* and *Preserving Habitat* and *Sure To Get In The Papers*. He'll love it!'

For a moment, Mr Haggerthwaite stared at her. Then his eyes lit up. 'Of course! A Wilderness Garden! But then there's lots of things I can do. We'll keep the trees and the grasses, of course. But we can clean up the lake and the stream – that will encourage birds and insects, and fish too. Not to mention frogs and toads. We can plant buddleia for the butterflies. And in spring we'll have bluebells—'

Mr Haggerthwaite was bursting with ideas. Jessica told her father she would read up on wild habitats, and Midge said he would help clean up the lake. Robbie said he would chop down anything that needed to be chopped. They spent the next hour happily making plans.

When they got home, they found Mrs Haggerthwaite in a good mood too. She was humming to herself, and there was a little smile playing at the corners of her mouth, funny stains on her fingers, and a smoky, charred smell in the air. And there was a look in her eye that said that Xandra, Friend of the Wind Spirits, had better look out.

Of course, Jessica did not really expect Mrs Haggerthwaite's Incantation to do anything. But part of her could not help hoping that Xandra would indeed be exposed as a fraud and a liar, and be forced to flee Bellstone in disgrace, taking horrible Agapanthus with her. 'Or, failing that,' said Jessica to Midge, 'a few boils on her nose would be nice.' But the next day Agapanthus was at school, looking as disdainful as ever, and if her mother had developed any boils she did not mention it.

So Jessica tried to forget about them, and to concentrate on her future TV career instead. But a few days later something happened which made that difficult. Miss Barnaby made an announcement.

'Today, we have a treat in store. As you know, from time to time, we invite parents with particularly interesting jobs to come and talk to the school about them.' (Jessica frowned: she could not remember such a thing and nor, from their puzzled expressions, could anyone else.) 'And this afternoon, Agapanthus's mother, Xandra – err – Friend of the Wind Spirits, will be telling us all about what it's like to – err – well, to be a friend of the Wind Spirits. So, you can all be thinking of questions you'd like to ask her. Now, fetch out your maths books, please.'

'It's just typical,' complained Jessica to Robbie after lunch, when they were doing art, and Miss Barnaby was busy at the other end of the room. 'They've never asked *my* parents to come in and talk about their jobs.'

'Nor my dad,' Robbie agreed.

'Well, I shall have a few questions for that Xandra anyway,' said Jessica grimly. 'One: What is a Wind Spirit? Two: How do you become its Friend? Three—'

'By the way,' said Robbie quickly (he had a feeling Jessica could go on for some time). 'I've got that address for you. The TV producer my dad knows.'

He produced a piece of paper and sent it spinning across the table, where it shot over the edge and onto the floor. Jessica was about to pick it up, but somebody got there first.

'Really, Robbie, Jessica,' said Agapanthus. 'You shouldn't be sending notes. I've a good mind to tell Miss Barnaby.'

'Give it back!' Jessica snapped.

'Private is it? Maybe it's a love letter!' Jessica made to snatch the paper out of Agapanthus's hand, but Agapanthus darted around the other side of the table. As she examined the piece of paper her face fell. '*Bill Mycroft, Mind-Boggling TV*,' she read aloud. 'Who's that?'

'Wouldn't you like to know?'

'You're not thinking of going on the *telly*, are you, Jessie?' Agapanthus sounded as if she thought this a very good joke.

'Yes, I am, actually,' said Jessica. 'And don't call me *Jessie*.'

Agapanthus stared at her. Then she began to giggle. 'You must be joking—' She would have said more, but Robbie skidded into her, rather as if he were doing a tackle on the football pitch (a dirty tackle at that) and lunged for the piece of paper. Agapanthus managed to hold onto it, but fell backwards, taking a jar of paint-filled water with her. Jessica and Robbie thought it was worth a hundred pounds at least, seeing the expression on her face as she sat there, soaked and gasping. It was certainly worth the telling off Miss Barnaby gave them afterwards for laughing at her.

* * *

It seemed that the whole school was going to be watching Xandra's presentation. Jessica was standing with her class, waiting for the younger kids to file into the Assembly Hall, when she spotted Midge. She also spotted a familiar brown lump sitting on his shoulder.

'Give him back!' Midge grabbed but it was too late. Jessica was already tucking Liverwort into her cardigan pocket.

'I *told* you not to bring him to school. You'll lose him again!'

Midge scowled, but was forced to follow the rest of his class into the hall. 'I can't believe Midge sometimes,' Jessica said to Robbie. 'Imagine if Liverwort escaped!'

'Could be a laugh,' said Robbie, grinning. 'And by the way, don't worry about that address. I'll get it back.'

'Thanks,' said Jessica. And with that they began filing into the hall.

The pupils of West Bellstone Primary had never seen anything like Xandra, Friend of the Wind Spirits. She was already standing on the platform, looking even more exotic than usual, especially next to Miss Barnaby in her sensible cardigan and skirt. Xandra herself was wearing a particularly vivid pink tunic, a kind of boiled-sweet colour, with roses in her hair, and was staring into the distance as if she was in a world of her own. There was a chair nearby which was clearly intended for her, as it was draped in pink fabric too. This was noted with some disappointment by those who had heard about Xandra's habits and had hoped she would be standing on her head.

Miss Barnaby finished her introductions and scuttled to the back of the hall. Then Xandra stepped forward. Her dreamy look had vanished.

'Greetings, children,' she began in a low melodious voice that somehow reached the back of the room. 'I make no apologies for dragging you from your classrooms this afternoon. Of course, you were learning many important things there. Important, if rather *dull*, things like arithmetic,

science and spelling. But there are more important things than those! Today, you will really learn something! For I shall tell you about the Wind Spirits. I will introduce you to their world – a world full of enchantment and mystery. Listen, children: life will never be the same again!'

Some of the teachers present did not look too impressed by this beginning. As for the kids, about half of them (mostly girls) 'oohed' and 'ahhed' while the rest (mostly boys) snorted or giggled or just sat and stared.

Xandra held up a hand for silence. 'What is a Wind Spirit, you will be wondering. Now, without more ado, I want everyone to close their eyes and listen, really listen, for the Wind Spirits . . .'

Everybody (even the gigglers) did as they were told – everybody except Jessica, that is. Everyone else shut their eyes tight and listened as hard as they

could – not that there was much to hear but the traffic outside, and Xandra wailing, 'Come Wind Spirits, come!' But Jessica was peeping.

She was still not sure exactly what she thought of Xandra – especially when she looked so glamorous and exciting. But Jessica was a scientist, and she liked to scrutinise all the available evidence. There was no way she was going to close her eyes.

She watched Xandra sit down on her pink-draped chair. Then Xandra gazed mistily into the distance – but not so mistily that she was not able to position herself for the photographer who suddenly leapt out from nowhere and started taking photographs.

Huh! thought Jessica. *What's he doing? He doesn't look like a Wind Spirit to me.*

Then, suddenly, Xandra stopped wailing, the photographer stopped clicking, and for a moment there was complete silence, with none of the usual scuffling of feet. Everybody waited, tense and expectant.

And then they heard it. A whispering sound, like the wind makes, passing through leaves.

'It's the Wind Spirits!' hissed someone.

'Must be!'

'Course it is!'

Then it faded. For a moment they thought they

had only imagined it. But, suddenly, there it was again – a rustling, a soft sigh, the sound of something breathing. Were there really Wind Spirits amongst them, flying about the room?

All this time Jessica had been staring hard at the platform. It seemed to her that the strange noises were coming from there. And she noticed something else, too. Xandra's foot was moving. It seemed to be tapping on the floor. Or perhaps it was moving something, behind that billowing pink fabric—

'Hey!' yelled Jessica. And as everyone watched, astonished, she went running to the platform and swung herself up. Before Xandra could stop her, she had swept aside the mountains of pink fabric around the chair and revealed – a tape recorder.

'Look!' said Jessica. 'It was her all the time! She was working it with her foot!'

Such was the commotion of kids shouting, it was impossible to hear anything else. Jessica was grinning, and Xandra was red with anger. For a moment, she did not look at all vague and dreamy. 'I suppose you think you've been very clever?' she hissed at Jessica, under cover of the noise.

'Yes,' said Jessica.

'Well, after all, Mrs – err – Wind Spirit,' gasped Miss Barnaby, who had arrived panting onto the

platform, and overheard. 'I think you have some explaining to do.'

For a fraction of a second Xandra looked at a loss. Then a sad, misunderstood expression appeared on her face. 'Don't you see? I was playing these sounds to attract the Wind Spirits. These are *their* sounds, after all. They make them feel at home. I never thought anybody would think they were made by the Wind Spirits themselves. Of course, now that there has been this *rude* interruption –' she gazed reproachfully at Jessica – 'I very much doubt we will be able to attract them back again.'

'Oh dear,' said Miss Barnaby. 'How unfortunate. It really was most *inconsiderate* of you, Jessica.'

Jessica gasped. 'You don't mean you *believe* her, do you?'

But this was exactly what Miss Barnaby meant. Jessica, still protesting, was forced to return to her seat. And for the next ten minutes, everybody sat absolutely silent, all over again, while Xandra tried in vain to summon the Wind Spirits once more.

'The atmosphere has been ruined,' Xandra announced, tragically, at last. 'The Spirits have fled. But never mind – dear, *dear* children. Let me answer your questions instead.'

A forest of arms appeared. Most of the kids did not know what to make of Xandra, but they certainly had plenty of things they wanted to ask her. And what most people wanted to know, like Jessica, was exactly what a Wind Spirit *was*. Xandra had quite a lot to say about this. She talked about

there being 'more things in this world than eye or ear can tell', about 'beings beyond our ken' and 'entities without body or breath'. But at the end of it, nobody had any more clue about what a Wind Spirit was than they'd had before.

Xandra had been deliberately ignoring Jessica's arm, but during a lull in the discussion Jessica decided to ask her question anyway. She stood up. 'These Wind Spirits,' she said loudly. 'If they're really there, flying about, then why is there no *evidence* that they're there? I mean, why are there no photographs or film of them?'

For a moment, it seemed Xandra would ignore her. Then she murmured, 'As I've said, *there are more things in this world—*'

'*—than eye or ear can tell,*' Jessica finished for her. 'I heard you the first time. But that's not good enough. I'm a scientist, and I think things should be *proved*. If you don't give us any evidence, then why should we believe that Wind Spirits exist?'

Two spots of colour appeared in Xandra's cheeks. 'Where is your childhood intuition?' she demanded. 'I appeal to all you children! Do you not feel in your hearts that there are Wind Spirits, flying through the skies?'

The children of West Bellstone Primary gaped at her.

Jessica said, 'And that's another thing. This flying business. You've talked today about flying with the Wind Spirits, and that's what it says in your leaflet, too. Are you seriously telling us that you can fly?'

'Friendship with Wind Spirits brings many marvellous powers.'

'Marvellous? But it's impossible! Nobody can fly. Haven't you heard of gravity?'

'What is gravity but a word?' asked Xandra dreamily.

'It's a force, that's what it is! And it pulls you down!'

'It means nothing to the Wind Spirits. Nor to their friends.'

This was so ridiculous that Jessica lost patience entirely. 'Then you ought to be on telly!' she told Xandra rudely. 'If you can really fly, you'd make your fortune.'

Everyone giggled. Miss Barnaby was signalling to Jessica that she should be quiet, and let someone else ask a question, but nobody was paying her any attention, least of all Jessica. But as it happened, it was Agapanthus who spoke next.

'Actually, Mum, *Jessica's* planning to go on telly herself,' she said in a high, clear voice.

Jessica felt the colour rise in her face as everyone stared at her. 'So what if I am?' she asked rashly.

'That's lovely, dear,' said Xandra, 'although I wouldn't have thought you were quite right for TV. They like people to be stylish you know.' She stared pointedly at Jessica. 'Some new clothes might not come amiss.' She laughed – she was in charge of the situation now. 'But never mind that. You were asking about flying. How can I describe it to you? It is a wonderful feeling – to be part of the air, a creature of the wild – filled with love for all creation—'

Suddenly, she stopped short, staring hard at the ground. Everyone began to wriggle, trying to see what she was looking at. All they could see were Xandra's feet, bare as usual, with sparkling pink toe-nails. But even as they watched, a small brown lump appeared from behind her ankle. It crawled onto her foot.

'Ugh!' shrieked Xandra. 'How beastly – how disgusting – it's alive!'

It seemed that Xandra's love of all creation did not include toads. For, of course, it was Liverwort. Somehow he had escaped, probably when Jessica had leapt up onto the stage.

Jessica and Midge both ran forward, but before they could do anything, Xandra flicked her foot, and Liverwort went hurtling through the air – right over the astonished heads of the pupils of West

Bellstone Primary. He uttered a startled croak as he
went.

Robbie said later that Xandra must play football
in her spare time. It was certainly quite a kick.
Liverwort went arcing through the air and into the

audience, where his arrival caused a quite amazing amount of havoc, given that he was, after all, only a toad, not very big, and not very nippy on his feet. At least a third of those present (including Jessica and Midge of course) flung themselves towards him, desperate to catch him, while another third (those who were particularly afraid of toads) tried desperately to get away. The remaining third sat tight, laughing their heads off, and tripping up everybody else. Under the circumstances, even though all Liverwort could manage was a slow crawl, it took a surprisingly long time for him to be caught, during which several people had hysterics, and one of the smallest kids threw up. A bag of leaflets, which Xandra had brought for the kids to take home to their parents, went flying into the air like confetti. On top of everything else, the photographer was darting about taking shots. The flashes from his camera terrified Liverwort, who crawled behind Miss Barnaby's handbag and, for a time, disappeared altogether.

It was Robbie who finally caught him, with a flying leap that took Liverwort away from right under the noses of two other boys. He waved him triumphantly in the air, then restored him to Jessica. Liverwort gave a sad croak and hid his head. He had not had an enjoyable afternoon.

Chapter Four

By the time order was restored, school was over. Miss Barnaby kept Jessica behind. She forbade her from bringing Liverwort to school ever again and also said that Jessica had 'ruined a most interesting presentation'. She refused to listen to Jessica's comments about how Xandra should be reported to the RSPCA for cruelty to toads. Jessica left in a fine temper, but while she was fetching her bag from the cloakroom next door, she overheard Miss Barnaby getting a telling off herself.

Mrs Oakley, the head teacher, was not pleased. 'The whole event was a disgrace,' she told Miss Barnaby. 'As you know, I had grave doubts from the start. And especially having photographers from the *Gazette* present! I only agreed because Mr Flotsam telephoned me himself, and he has a son at this school. I have just been speaking to him and luckily he has agreed not to publish the pictures – otherwise I am sure we would see the whole fiasco plastered across the *Gazette*!'

Jessica left the school feeling quite sorry for Miss Barnaby. She suspected that Xandra had bullied Miss Barnaby into agreeing to the talk. (It was quite easy to bully Miss Barnaby, Jessica had often done it herself.) But she was absolutely furious with Xandra. 'It's amazing you weren't killed!' Jessica told Liverwort, who was back in her pocket again. Liverwort croaked faintly. Jessica now strongly suspected that Xandra was a fraud, who had only offered to give the talk in the first place as a publicity exercise.

It was very worrying that she should have got Mr Flotsam and the *Gazette* on her side.

'Robbie should have warned me,' said Jessica aloud.

She walked on, still brooding on this, and feeling more and more angry, when she caught sight of a group of boys playing football in Bellstone Public Park. One of the goalies was Robbie Flotsam.

'Hey!' Rather out of breath, Jessica arrived behind him and prodded him in the back.

Robbie spun round, about to punch whoever it

was very hard on the nose. Then he saw it was Jessica. 'Oh, hello,' he said. 'I wouldn't stand there if I was you. That coat's the post. Someone might hit it.'

'Never mind that,' said Jessica. 'Did you know that photographer was from the *Gazette*?'

'I guessed it might be.'

'What!'

'Yeah, Dad told me they're doing an article about Xandra. She came round to see him specially.'

'What!' Jessica shrieked again. 'You knew that and you didn't tell me!'

Robbie shrugged. 'I forgot. Anyway, I was wondering when you would show up. I ran home after school and fetched that address for you. I couldn't get it off Agapanthus 'cause she went home with her mum.' He handed her the bit of paper.

'Never mind that!' Jessica yelled. And she was just telling him exactly what she thought of him, and his father too, for falling in with Xandra's plans, when the football came flying out of nowhere and hit her full in the stomach. She punched it away – unfortunately, right into the path of the other team's attacker. It was Sam Harris, who was famous for panicking in front of goal, but even he couldn't miss a sitter like that.

'Goal!' yelled his delighted team-mates.

'That was your fault!' yelled Robbie, turning on Jessica.

'I don't care!' Jessica shouted. 'You make me sick!' And she turned and made for home.

For the next few days, Jessica did not speak to Robbie and he did not speak to her. Jessica was too busy helping her father after school, and doing research into the Wilderness Garden, to feel lonely. She also sent off copies of her letter to the BBC and ITV, as well as the address that Robbie had given her. But despite all this activity, by the end of the week she could not help noticing that Robbie was looking rather miserable. He spent a lot of time prowling about by himself in the playground, snarling at anyone who spoke to him, and he was in continual trouble in class. As he seemed to be really suffering, Jessica began to consider talking to him again, especially as, so far, no story had appeared about Xandra in the *Bellstone Gazette*.

On Friday, she waited for him near the gates after school. He appeared, and she was just stepping forward to say hello when Agapanthus came running up.

'Oh Robbie,' she said, 'you haven't forgotten that I'm coming home with you today, have you?' And

to Jessica's astonishment – and fury – they passed out of the gates together.

It was true that Robbie did not look particularly happy about it, but this did not lessen his treachery in Jessica's eyes.

'That creep!' she told Midge who was nearby. 'That toad!'

'There's nothing wrong with toads.'

'That weasel, then!'

Midge shrugged. 'You're jealous.'

'I am not! Those Flotsams are in league with Xandra against us!'

'Well, I'm going to meet Dad. Do you want to come?'

'Absolutely not!' said Jessica. 'I'm going home!' And she stormed off.

Midge set off alone, careful to keep Robbie and Agapanthus at a distance. They seemed to be ignoring each other, he noticed. When they reached the hotel, Robbie and Agapanthus disappeared inside and Midge went scooting into the grounds where he found Mr Haggerthwaite by the lake.

'Hello there, Midge,' said Mr Haggerthwaite. He was wearing long waders, and was knee deep in water. Despite this, he was looking extremely cheerful. 'Look at all this weed I've cleared away! The place is coming back to life. I've counted sixteen frogs already.'

'But has Mr Flotsam agreed to a Wilderness Garden?'

'I should get the go-ahead today. I gave him the final plans yesterday, and he said he'd get back to me this afternoon. Then I'll get some of those lads I've got working on the rose gardens down here, and we'll really see some changes!'

Mr Haggerthwaite went back to work, and Midge got out his sketchbook and began to sketch a pair of moorhens. He soon lost track of time. It was a while before he noticed some rustling in the reeds – and a strange, snapping noise.

Midge went to investigate. What he found surprised him very much. He went in search of Mr Haggerthwaite but found him deep in conversation with Mr Flotsam. And they were not alone. Beside them stood a fair-haired woman, in a pink tunic. Midge's jaw dropped. What, he wondered, was Xandra, Friend of the Wind Spirits, doing in the grounds of Mr Flotsam's hotel?

'As I said, I'm absolutely delighted with your plans, Tom,' boomed Mr Flotsam. 'Except – well – I was talking to Xandra here, and she's had an idea too. Xandra is of a mystical persuasion – a bit like your lady wife – and she thought we might incorporate some – err – mystical elements into your designs. Mystical elements – seems they're all the rage.'

There was a brief pause. Then: 'Is that so?' said Mr Haggerthwaite.

'Oh yes,' murmured Xandra. 'Think, Mr Haggerthwaite! Through this garden we can create a channel for the Spirits to enter Bellstone!'

There was another pause. Then: 'Is that so?' said

89

Mr Haggerthwaite again. Midge could tell he was not impressed. Mr Haggerthwaite had to listen to enough 'magical clap trap' (as, out of the hearing of his wife, he secretly called it) at home, without having to listen to the same kind of things from strangers. And he never liked it when 'amateurs' started interfering with his gardening.

Mr Flotsam, on the other hand, looked very impressed indeed. He was eating up Xandra's every word. There were certainly plenty of these, as she burbled on about 'positive energies' and 'beneficial influences'. But what it all seemed to boil down to was that she wanted to build a big pyramid of pink rocks in the middle of the rose garden. This, she said, would form a Spiritual Vortex through which the Wind Spirits could enter Bellstone.

'What! A pile of rocks in my rose garden?' burst out Mr Haggerthwaite.

'Not just any rocks – special rocks, dedicated to the Spirits,' murmured Xandra. 'And they have to be placed in the rose garden. That is where the Spiritual Planes converge.'

'Well, couldn't they converge somewhere else? Like the vegetable garden, for instance? That pile of rocks is going to look plain daft among my roses.'

Xandra began to explain at length why this was impossible. Midge suddenly spotted Robbie

Flotsam emerging from the woods. Agapanthus was with him and they both looked fed up.

Robbie brightened when he saw Midge. 'I'm supposed to be looking after this bunch of fun,' he said, indicating Agapanthus. 'But I've had enough. D'you want to play computer games?'

'Not just now,' said Midge. Then he had a thought. He said in a low voice, 'Do you know where I could find a big box? And some – some sardines?'

Robbie stared at him.

'It's like this,' said Midge. 'You see – I've found something.'

He began to whisper. Once he understood, Robbie agreed to help and to keep the secret too. And of course he knew how to obtain everything Midge needed. The two of them went off together, ignoring Agapanthus, who had been trying to listen to their conversation while pretending not to, and who now tried to follow them, but gave up, squawking indignantly, when she found herself up to her ankles in mud. When they got back they found her sitting on the fallen log, sulking.

The three adults were still deep in discussion.

'Now, Tom,' Mr Flotsam was saying. 'Don't give me your answer now. Take some time to mull it over. But I have to say, I'm very keen on Xandra's suggestions. I don't think they'll spoil your designs at all. But you're the professional. It's your decision. Stop by at the hotel on your way home, and tell me what you think.'

Then he and Xandra set off towards the hotel, taking Agapanthus and Robbie with them.

Mr Haggerthwaite and Midge stared at each other.

'What am I going to do?' asked Mr Haggerthwaite.

Midge's first idea was that Mr Haggerthwaite should say that he would have nothing to do with Xandra's crazy ideas. But Mr Haggerthwaite said it was not so simple. They sat on the fallen log by the side of the lake, Mr Haggerthwaite produced a bag of peppermints, and while they munched he explained his dilemma.

'Of course I don't want piles of rock and goodness knows what else cluttering up the garden. And my first thought was to tell her to be off, and to take her Spiritual Vortex with her! But then I thought – what about your mother?'

'Mum? What's it got to do with her?'

'This Xandra is her friend. You heard her say so. The very first time she met her – she said she was going to be a friend.'

'I suppose that's true,' Midge admitted.

'So, if I turn down her new friend's ideas point blank – well, she won't like that. She's loyal, your mother is. It's one of her best qualities,' he added fondly.

'Yes,' said Midge, 'and a rotten temper is one of her worst qualities.'

'She can be a bit hasty,' admitted Mr Haggerthwaite. 'And the fact is I don't want to spark off a fight with her. Not now. Not over something as silly as a pile of rocks.'

Midge stared at his feet. He felt cold all over and there was a strange rushing noise in his ear. He had almost forgotten his secret fear – that the arrival of Xandra, Friend of the Wind Spirits, would somehow stir things up between his parents, and cause them to fall out. He had pushed it to the back of his mind. But, he discovered now, that did not mean it had gone away.

There was something else, too. Underlying his fear was the secret conviction that if his parents fell out, his father might leave home. He had walked out once before, after all, when Mrs Haggerthwaite had decided to become a professional witch. He had soon come home again, and everything had been sorted out: in fact, Mr and Mrs Haggerthwaite seemed happier than ever. They had hardly had a single argument since, which was amazing, for they

usually had some disagreement or other at least once a week. They were almost bound to, with Mrs Haggerthwaite so hot tempered, and Mr Haggerthwaite stubborn as a mule. But somehow, the longer it was since they had fallen out, the more nervous Midge became about what would happen when they did. And at the back of his mind had grown up a terrible fear: that if his parents did fall out, and Mr Haggerthwaite left home again, then this time he might not come back.

Midge had not even been able to tell Jessica about this. He reached out a hand automatically for Liverwort: somehow, the presence of the old toad always comforted him. But Liverwort was not there. After the rumpus at Xandra's presentation, even Midge had not dared to take him to school.

Midge swallowed. Then, keeping his voice as normal as possible, he began, 'Dad—' but somehow he could get no further.

'So, what do you think I should do, son?' asked Mr Haggerthwaite.

'Well,' Midge said carefully. 'It seems a shame to upset Mum. And what does a Vortex matter, after all?'

'That's what I think. I'll tell Bert that it's fine with me, and then I'll bite my lip while this Xandra goes rabbiting on with her strange ideas.' He sighed and shook his head. 'The things I do for your mother. And what she sees in that woman, I can't imagine.'

Still, they both felt more cheerful now that the decision was made. They walked up to the hotel together to find Mr Flotsam. And, although it still came hard, whenever Mr Haggerthwaite thought of that pile of rubble in the middle of his rosebeds, at least he knew it was in a good cause: the peace and happiness of his family.

Meanwhile, Jessica marched home in a very bad mood indeed. She was determined to do something to show Xandra and the Flotsams what was what. And it was time she made some progress with her TV career. So she went to the telephone and called the number for Mind-Boggling TV – it was several days since she had sent them her letter, after all. Having listened to piped music for ages, she finally managed to talk to somebody in the children's department, but they just promised to send her a signed photograph of Lisa Singh, 'our latest hot new children's presenter'. They did not seem to understand that Jessica, far from being a fan of Lisa Singh, was actually after her job.

She slammed down the phone. She was planning to telephone the BBC next, but Mrs Haggerthwaite came out into the hall, in between clients, and caught her. 'Have you seen the state of our phone bill?' said Mrs Haggerthwaite, and sent her off to do her homework. Jessica fetched Liverwort for company, and went up to her room. But she did not get out her homework.

One of the things that had been niggling in

Jessica's mind was Xandra's comment about her appearance. Was it true that she was not stylish enough to be a TV star?

After studying the contents of her wardrobe, she had to admit that none of her clothes looked right for launching a media career. The problem, she thought gloomily, was her parents. Most of her things had either been chosen by Mr Haggerthwaite, who favoured clothes 'that would wash well and stand the mud', or Mrs Haggerthwaite, who seemed to think that her daughter should dress like a vampire. It was either jeans and jumpers, or long, shabby dresses with moth holes. Neither were exactly glamorous.

'It's no good!' Jessica declared furiously to Liverwort, contemplating herself in the mirror in a sagging purple dress that Mrs Haggerthwaite had bought at a jumble sale. 'I look all wrong!'

Jessica did not hear the

sound of voices below, nor the bang of the front door, as Mrs Haggerthwaite's last client left. Nor did she hear the thud of the *Bellstone Gazette* landing on the door mat a few moments later. But, preoccupied though she was, she could not help hearing the loud and piercing shriek that Mrs Haggerthwaite let out soon afterwards. Probably the whole street heard it.

'AAARGH!!!!'

'What is it?' yelled Jessica. She rushed out of her room and down the stairs, her progress not helped by the fact that as well as the long dress she was wearing a pair of stiletto shoes that Mrs Haggerthwaite had bought at the same jumble sale. Just before she got to the bottom of the stairs she caught her foot, tripped, and went careering straight into Mrs Haggerthwaite.

For a moment, there was only the sound of witch-like curses (Mrs Haggerthwaite) and muffled squawking (Jessica). By the time Jessica had rescued her shoes from the umbrella stand, Mrs Haggerthwaite was back on her feet again and waving a copy of the *Bellstone Gazette* at Jessica. 'That woman!' she snarled. 'That Xandra Wind Spirit!'

Jessica grabbed hold of the paper, and found herself staring at a gigantic picture of Xandra, sitting with her legs crossed. But, instead of sitting on the floor she was (though this Jessica could hardly believe) floating in midair.

'She isn't – flying!'

'Of course she isn't,' snapped Mrs Haggerthwaite. 'The whole thing is a trick, from beginning to end!'

The caption underneath the picture read *Xandra, Bellstone's Flying Star!*

Jessica began to skim through the article:

Mystic and Friend of the Spirits Comes to Bellstone . . . Beautiful and enigmatic, Xandra Wind Spirit spoke to our reporter, Pete Blakeley . . . 'I have a mission to help Bellstone discover its spiritual self,' she said . . . will be giving classes and guidance one-to-one . . . bunions, bad breath, acne and snoring can all be vanquished by adopting a more spiritual attitude, Xandra says . . .

Then Jessica's eyes fastened on two paragraphs, halfway down the page.

When asked how her spiritual approach compared to witchcraft, Xandra Wind Spirit laughed. 'Yes, I have met Bellstone's witch,' she said. 'But I'm bound to say I was not impressed. Witchcraft might have been all right in the fourteenth century, but the world has moved on. I would advise people to look to the World of the Spirits, not to silly potions and other hocus-pocus.'

Xandra added, 'Witches are supposed to fly, aren't they? But when did you last see a witch on a broomstick?'

She would not reveal her own secrets of flight – or levitation, as she prefers to call it. But she said that many years of communing with the World of the Spirits was necessary before achieving successful lift-off.

Then there was a bit about Xandra's very reasonable prices, and another bit about how communing with the Wind Spirits helped to maintain her clear and youthful skin, and finally a smarmy bit about '*what a wonderful addition to the cultural and spiritual life of Bellstone*' Xandra Wind Spirit was. ('Huh!' thought Jessica. 'She buttered you up all right, Pete Blakeley!') And that was it.

'I don't believe she can fly,' Jessica told her mother.

'Of course she can't! And how dare she insult us witches in that way. I'll tell you, it will be all the worse for her when my Incantation kicks in.'

'Exactly when is it going to kick in?' asked Jessica.

'These things don't work on a timetable, you know!' Mrs Haggerthwaite snapped. 'It's not like one of your scientific experiments.'

'I can see that,' said Jessica rashly. 'I mean, my experiments work.'

Mrs Haggerthwaite scowled at her. 'Never mind that!' And she strode to the door, obviously wanting to waste no time in finding Xandra and giving her a piece of her mind. But before she could get there, the door opened and Mr Haggerthwaite and Midge appeared.

'Well, hello,' said Mr Haggerthwaite. 'What's going on here?'

Mrs Haggerthwaite just thrust the *Bellstone Gazette* at him. He smoothed it out and stared at the picture of Xandra. 'Well, isn't that a coincidence?'

'What do you mean?' asked Mrs Haggerthwaite.

'Well, this is Xandra Whatsits. We were just speaking to her down at the hotel. We were discussing plans for the gardens with her, weren't we, Midge?'

Mr Haggerthwaite was still staring at the picture, which meant that he did not notice the expression on his wife's face. It was not a friendly expression. Her eyebrows lowered and her mouth disappeared into a thin, white line. In a tight voice she asked, 'And *why* were you talking about your plans for the gardens with her, may I ask? I mean, what can it possibly have to do with her?'

'Well, it turns out she's a friend of Bert Flotsam's. She's got some ideas and he's keen to adopt them. A Spiritual Vortex for the rose garden, for example. A very – err – *interesting* idea we thought, didn't we, Midge?'

Then, for the first time, Mr Haggerthwaite

caught sight of his wife's face. He took a quick step back.

'I don't believe it!' Mrs Haggerthwaite yelled.

'What don't you believe, dear?'

'My own husband! Turning traitor!'

'But I thought—'

'Now, if *I* dared to suggest anything for the hotel gardens I know exactly what would happen. *Keep your big nose out!* you would say. *You get on with your business, and leave me to get on with mine.* But when Miss Wind Spirit comes along, batting her eyelashes and spouting off all kinds of nonsense about a Spiritual Vortex, it's a different story.'

Jessica could not help wondering just what a Spiritual Vortex was. An ordinary vortex, she knew, was a whirlpool, or a moving spiral, which you might find in gases; but she did not see how you could have a vortex of *Spirits*. She was going to mention this but it was hard with her parents yelling so loudly.

'The trouble with you, Tom Haggerthwaite, is that you're a soft touch! That lying, scheming little minx! She wrapped you right round her finger!'

'That's not true!' Mr Haggerthwaite bawled. 'But I am soft – that's right enough! I only agreed to please you!'

Both Mr and Mrs Haggerthwaite were scarlet with anger. Mrs Haggerthwaite was stabbing her finger in the air every time she made a point, and Mr Haggerthwaite was banging his fist against his hand. Neither of them was listening to what the other one was saying, and neither of them noticed that Midge had gone white as skimmed milk. Jessica did. She wondered if he was going to throw up.

Suddenly, Midge gave a gasp, and went racing up the stairs. Mr and Mrs Haggerthwaite paid no attention as Jessica went hurtling after him, carrying her shoes for speed.

'What is it?' she cried. 'What's the matter?'

Midge was white and shaking. 'I can't bear it! I can't bear it if Dad – if Dad—' Then he broke away and ran into the bathroom, locking the door behind him.

Jessica stared after him. For a moment, her own thoughts seemed to be spinning in a vortex inside her head. Then they stopped whirling and everything became clear.

She raced downstairs and heaved herself up onto the banisters. It was a bit tricky, in her long dress, but she managed. For a moment she stood there, wobbling.

Then she bawled 'SHUT UP!' and threw her purple stilettos at them.

This caught their attention all right. They both gaped at her.

'Don't you see?' Jessica said. 'You're upsetting Midge. He hates quarrels. I think – I think he's afraid you're going to split up again.'

'Of course we're not going to split up,' said Mrs Haggerthwaite.

'Why on earth should he think that?' said Mr Haggerthwaite.

'Well, it's obvious, isn't it? Because you're both

stubborn and bad tempered, and you have stupid quarrels and say stupid things you don't mean, and then you won't back down. After all, that's why Dad moved out before. All because of a stupid quarrel about something that didn't matter anyway.'

Mr and Mrs Haggerthwaite looked ashamed.

'That's why I persuaded Mum not to make a fuss about Xandra Wind Spirit in the first place,' Jessica went on. 'Because Midge hates rows. I told her to try and be friends instead.'

'But that was the only reason I agreed to Xandra's ideas for the hotel gardens,' said Mr Haggerthwaite, surprised. 'Because I thought she was a friend of yours, Melly. Otherwise I'd have

told her what she could do with her Spiritual Vortex.'

They stared at each other.

'I think we should go and talk to Midge,' said Mrs Haggerthwaite.

They found Midge in the loft. He had crawled into the narrow space under the eaves, where there was not even a proper floor – only joists of wood with plaster in between. Jessica was not sure, because she could not really see in the dim light, but she thought he was crying. She crawled in after him along one of the joists, and Mr and Mrs Haggerthwaite crawled in too (or as much of them as would fit). Jessica held out Liverwort to Midge

who immediately seized him and clutched him to his chest.

'Go away,' said Midge.

'No!' said Jessica. 'They've come to say they're sorry.' She wriggled round in the small space and glared at her parents. 'Haven't you?' she demanded.

'Yes,' said Mr and Mrs Haggerthwaite meekly.

'And you're never going to split up – are you?'

'No,' agreed Mr and Mrs Haggerthwaite, even more meekly. And Mr Haggerthwaite said, 'Midge, it was just a quarrel. Really it was. We will never split up, I promise you.'

'So do I,' said Mrs Haggerthwaite. 'But,' she went on, 'we can't promise you not to have arguments. That's just the way we are.'

'I'm afraid so,' agreed Mr Haggerthwaite.

Jessica peered at Midge's small white face, which was all smudged with soot and tears. It seemed to her he was breathing more calmly, as Mrs Haggerthwaite said, 'You see, everybody has arguments sometimes. You must promise us that you won't think we're going to split up, just because we have a stupid argument.'

'Lots of people's parents don't argue,' said Midge.

Mr and Mrs Haggerthwaite looked downcast.

'Maybe they're better parents than we are, son,' said Mr Haggerthwaite gloomily.

'That's rubbish,' said Jessica firmly. She turned on Midge. 'Just because they argue, doesn't mean that they're not good parents. Anyway,' she added, 'you might as well make the best of it. Because they're the only ones we've got.'

For a brief second, Midge still looked white and haunted. Then his face broke into a grin. 'Yes, and I think they're just fine!'

'Of course we are!' cried Mrs Haggerthwaite in relief. 'Why, we're the best parents in the world!'

She flung her arms wide and crawled forward to give Midge a hug. Then she let out a squawk as her foot slipped off the joist and burst right through the ceiling of the room below.

Later that evening, Jessica and Midge sat together on the sofa watching TV. Midge was wrapped in a dressing gown and blanket, and drinking hot milk. He felt warm and reassured. Liverwort was perched on his shoulder and Jessica sat beside him, dressed now in her ordinary jeans and T-shirt. From above them came the faint sounds of Mr and Mrs Haggerthwaite as they argued about the hole in their bedroom ceiling.

'They really won't split up, you know,' said Jessica, after a particularly loud bellow.

'I know,' said Midge. He grinned at her, a half-embarrassed and half-grateful grin.

They watched a chat show and then the news came on. Midge listened with one ear to the newsreader, and with the other to Jessica who was explaining how much better she would do it if she was a TV presenter, and complaining because there were never enough science stories.

The local news came on. Suddenly, they both sat bolt upright.

'. . . and now, a report from Bellstone, where an emissary from the Spirits has recently arrived among the local population . . .' And there was Xandra looking extremely pleased with herself.

Jessica gave a squawk of indignation. 'Why's she on telly? And –' a note of absolute outrage crept into her voice – 'what's *she* doing?' For sitting next to Xandra was Agapanthus, smirking away like anything.

'So, why have you come to Bellstone?' the interviewer asked.

'I feel the time has come for the people of Bellstone to discover their true selves,' cooed Xandra. 'All of us have a deep spiritual core, but the people of Bellstone have forgotten this. For some reason, malevolent forces have not allowed the Spirits to thrive in Bellstone. But an experienced

Spirit Friend, like myself, will soon be able to coax them back again . . .'

'And how are you going to do that?'

'I will be running classes. And, thanks to the vision and encouragement of Mr Bert Flotsam, I will be transforming the grounds of his Luxury Hotel into a Haven for the Spirits. I shall be constructing a Spiritual Vortex through which the Spirits will enter Bellstone and fill it with their marvellous presence . . . it will be ideal for people coming on weekend breaks . . .'

'I notice she didn't say anything about the riot she caused at our school,' said Jessica, as the item ended. She felt bitter. All the work she had put into getting on TV – and they had beaten her to it! 'At least Agapanthus didn't get to say anything. I'd never have heard the last of it.'

'Dad won't be pleased,' Midge observed. '*He's* meant to be in charge of Mr Flotsam's gardens, not Xandra. She makes it sound like the whole thing is down to her. And Mum won't like it either. I bet *she's* the malevolent force. Still,' he added, 'at least they'll be on the same side for once.'

'Huh!' said Jessica. The anger was building up inside her and it burst out. 'This is too much! First that woman almost kills Liverwort, then she gets in the papers and now she's on television. Well, I'll show her! Just you wait and see.'

'Oh,' said Midge. Suddenly, he no longer felt warm and reassured. 'How will you do that?'

'I don't know. But I'll think of something. And I'll tell you something else. This is all those Flotsams' fault! Mr Flotsam must have got her into the *Gazette* – and on TV too. You wait till I see Robbie!'

She stormed out of the room. Midge sighed, then picked up Liverwort. 'I think we're in for a bad time, old friend,' he told the toad.

Chapter Five

Jessica was determined to get her revenge on Xandra and Agapanthus. She felt the best way to do so was by appearing on a bigger and better TV show. But until she could arrange this, it would at least relieve her feelings to have things out with Robbie Flotsam. Jessica believed in taking immediate action on her ideas so, since she could not go round to the hotel that night, she set her alarm for an early hour the next morning.

When the time came, it was harder than she had expected to drag herself out of bed, but she crept downstairs at last, pleased but surprised to find that nobody else was awake before her. She left a note for Midge, saying she would see him at school, and was sneaking out of the house when she noticed a letter had arrived addressed to her.

Dear Miss Hasslegaite,

Thank you for writing to us with your ideas for science programmes for children. However, we feel most kids get more than enough science at school, without watching it at home too! I hope you will enjoy the two new Children's TV series that we do have planned especially for your age group, Popworld! *and* Amazing Celebrity Pets!

You mentioned dinosaurs in your letter. You may also enjoy our cartoon series for younger children, Bonzo the Baby Brontosaurus *(Saturday lunchtimes).*

Yours

Trudy McFadden

(New Programming, Kids Mind-Boggling TV)

P.S. Bill Mycroft passed your letter to me.

'Huh!' said Jessica. '*Popworld*, indeed!'

She was livid. She had spent ages thinking up good ideas for science programmes, and this stupid letter was all she had to show for it. Whereas somebody like Xandra (and, even more annoyingly, Agapanthus) could get themselves on television just by spouting a load of nonsense that didn't even make sense. Of course, there were still the other TV companies to hear from, but she had based most of her hopes on Mind-Boggling TV, who had studios nearby. Jessica continued to brood about it as she ran along the early-morning streets, and by the time she had passed into the grounds of Flotsam's Hotel she was in a terrible temper.

She hid behind a yew tree to wait for Robbie. When he set off for school she would leap out and then give him a piece of her mind!

A few minutes later, Robbie did appear but, to Jessica's surprise, he set off into the gardens.

She followed, and soon realised he was going towards the Wilderness Garden – or what Mr Haggerthwaite intended for the Wilderness Garden. Probably it was going to be the Spirits' Croquet Pitch now, Jessica thought crossly.

It was still looking wild enough: early-morning sunlight sparkled on the dew that still rested on the grass; roses nodded amongst the brambles; and foxgloves stood up like purple spears in the undergrowth. As Jessica made her way a couple of startled rabbits came racing out, almost from under her feet. She found Robbie staring moodily across the lake.

'Hey!' she said, confronting him hands on hips. 'Have you forgotten about school?'

'Have you forgotten it's Saturday?'

Jessica went red. 'Oh. Well then, why aren't you asleep? Or watching TV?'

It was a good question. Robbie Flotsam was not known as a nature-lover; he did not rise early on weekends to hunt for wild flowers or listen to the dawn chorus.

Robbie scowled. 'Why shouldn't I be here? It's my dad's garden, I can come here if I want to.'

'That's what you think. You'd better watch out. Or you might bump into a load of Wind Spirits.'

Jessica sat down on the fallen log. For some reason, she did not feel angry any more. Perhaps it was because it was such a beautiful morning, and the garden was so still and peaceful. Or perhaps it was because there was something strangely subdued about Robbie himself. He came and sat down beside her, and now she could see that he was looking very pale, and there were dark smudges beneath his eyes. In fact, he looked rather like Midge had last night.

Suddenly, Jessica felt sorry for him. 'What's up?' she asked.

'Nothing.'

'I'm not stupid. What are you doing here?'

Robbie shoved his hands into his pockets. 'Can't a person come out for a bit of peace and quiet, without you turning up? I just wanted to be by myself. To think.'

'But why?'

'It's none of your business.'

'Course it is. We're friends aren't we?'

'Are we?' Robbie lifted his chin and stared at her accusingly.

'Course we are!' Then a thought struck her. 'Is that what you're upset about? Because you thought we weren't friends?' Secretly, she could not help feeling flattered that he should have missed her so much.

'No!' said Robbie, squashing that idea. 'It's nothing to do with that. It's – well, it's to do with my dad.'

'What's he done now?'

Robbie hunched his shoulders. 'He's – well, do you promise not to tell anybody?' Jessica promised. 'Well – he's got a girlfriend. And – and I'm afraid they're going to get married!' He dug his hands even further into his pockets, and scowled hard at the ground.

'Wow,' said Jessica, taken aback. After all, why would anyone want to marry Mr Flotsam? True, he was rich, and his wife would be able to live in this beautiful hotel; but he also spent all his time telling everyone how rich and successful he was (which got very boring) and he was a bully and not really interested in anyone but himself. Jessica had always felt sorry for Robbie, having to put up with him.

Spirits. Who did you think I meant?'

'I don't know!' Jessica leapt to her feet, sending another pair of rabbits hurtling for cover. 'It could have been anybody! But that Xandra Wind Spirit! Eugh! Why didn't you say so?'

Robbie stared at her in astonishment. 'But I just did!'

'No you didn't! I mean – anyway, hasn't she done enough? Getting herself all over the telly, and kicking Liverwort, and trying to ruin my mum's business *and* my dad's garden – *and* sending her revolting daughter to ruin our school! Now she has the nerve to nobble your dad! And if they get married, she'll never be out of the *Gazette*, I know it! Or off the telly. Your dad probably knows someone who will give the woman her own TV series!'

'That would be bad,' Robbie agreed. 'Although Dad did say he had nothing to do with her being on the news last night.'

'I don't believe him!' Jessica screeched. 'How will I ever get on the telly with her hogging it? Well, I've had enough! I'm not going to let her get away with this!'

Robbie stared at her. He felt rather confused at the turn the conversation had taken. Although it definitely seemed a turn for the better. 'So, does this mean I don't have to be nice to her, after all?' he asked hopefully.

'It's the last thing you should do! Otherwise she'll end up as your stepmother – and how would you like that? Do you know your problem, Robbie?' said Jessica severely. 'You're too soft!'

Robbie gaped. He had been accused of many things in his time ('rowdy troublemaker' it had said on his last report) but he had never been accused of being soft before.

'What should I do, then?' he asked.

'Help me, of course,' snapped Jessica. 'We'll show that Xandra what's what!'

Jessica's thirst for revenge grew still stronger on Monday, as Agapanthus told everyone who would listen that her TV appearance was 'the most marvellous and amazing experience of my entire life'. After she had finished describing for the twentieth time the exact shade of nail varnish she had worn, Jessica finally lost patience.

'It's not as if you even said anything,' she snapped, 'you just sat there, like a sausage. Anyway, you only got on TV because your mum's been cosying up to Mr Flotsam.'

'Actually, we got on TV because of you, Jessica,' said Agapanthus sweetly.

Jessica gasped. 'What do you mean?'

'You remember the name on that bit of paper Robbie gave you? Bill Mycroft? Well, I showed it my mum, and she phoned him, and he was dead interested. He told the news team about us *and* he says he's going to make a documentary now, all

about the Spiritual Vortex that Mum's building in the hotel gardens.'

Jessica was furious. She stomped off in disgust. But the conversation gave her the glimmerings of an idea. Bill Mycroft couldn't make a TV programme about a Spiritual Vortex which wasn't there – now could he?

She continued brooding on this over dinner, while Mr Haggerthwaite was complaining to the rest of the family about how much Xandra was disrupting his work. Mrs Haggerthwaite had tried to persuade him to tell Mr Flotsam that he had changed his mind about Xandra's plans, but Mr Haggerthwaite had refused. He was a man of strong principles, and did not believe in going back on his word. But this did not mean that he enjoyed watching Xandra interfering in his garden. 'Mess everywhere, and one of the roses trampled,' he reported glumly. 'And now she's talking about wind chimes in the cedar trees and a Fountain of Eternal Youth in the lily pond. Where will it end?'

Jessica pursed her lips. She could see that she would have to act fast, before it was too late.

Jessica could get a lot done in a short time. A couple of days later found her sitting next to Robbie on the fallen log by the lake, reading aloud from a typewritten list headed, *AIM: Stop Xandra!*

'One: Surveillance. That means spying,' she added for Robbie's benefit. 'We've got to know when they've finished setting up the Vortex. And when the TV cameras are due. So you must listen in to your dad's phone calls, Robbie, and I'll question my dad. Two: equipment. We'll need gloves, spades, sacks—'

She broke off. Was it her imagination, or could she hear a rustling noise? Maybe Xandra was prowling about, looking for a site for her next Vortex . . .

'Did you hear something?' she whispered to Robbie. He shook his head and she was just turning back to her notes, when—

'Gotcha!' Midge leapt out of the bushes.

'Eeek!' Jessica almost dropped her papers. 'What d'you think you're up to?' she demanded. 'Jumping out of bushes and scaring the living daylights out of us?'

'Espionage,' said Midge smugly. 'You're not the only one who knows about it. I could tell you were up to something. Sneaking about, typing away, and whispering with Robbie in corners of the playground. What's going on?'

Jessica and Robbie exchanged glances. 'We might as well tell him,' said Robbie. 'We could do with another pair of hands.'

Jessica nodded and handed Midge a piece of paper. He considered it, then read aloud, '*Stage One – dismantle Wortex*. What's a Wortex?'

'*Vortex*, not Wortex. The V on the typewriter's started jamming.'

'You should get a computer, they're miles better,' put in Robbie helpfully. 'I've got a fantastic one. And when Dad updates the computers for the hotel, I'll get an even better one.'

'That's nice,' grated Jessica. It seemed very unfair

that Robbie, who would only play games on it anyway, should get a brand new computer. 'Now can we get back to the plan?'

In the end, it was easier just to tell Midge what they intended to do. 'We're going to dismantle the Vortex,' Jessica explained. 'Then when the TV crew turn up to film Xandra she'll look a right idiot.'

Midge soon understood all the details, but that did not mean he was convinced. 'But how can we hide a Vortex?' he objected, and added: 'We'll get into terrible trouble.' Midge thought Jessica's plan went too far.

(Unlike Robbie, who thought it did not go far enough. He had tried unsuccessfully to persuade Jessica that they should blow up the Vortex.

'Where could we get explosives?' asked Jessica scathingly.

'We could make them,' said Robbie hopefully. 'It would be an interesting scientific experiment.')

What eventually persuaded Midge was the fact that Xandra was planning to take all the credit for the hotel gardens, when all the hard work had been done by Mr Haggerthwaite.

'But I still think we're going to get caught,' he added.

'Not if we get up really early,' said Jessica. 'About five o'clock, I thought. Then we'll all meet over here—'

'Mum and Dad will be suspicious if we get up early.'

'We'll tell them we've taken up jogging.' Jessica glared at Midge, who did not dare to point out the unlikelihood of this.

'But what shall we do with all the rocks from the Vortex?' asked Robbie. 'If we don't blow them up, that is.'

'Put them in the rockery,' said Jessica.

'Dad's bound to notice a load of new rocks appearing in his rockery,' said Midge. 'Especially pink ones.'

There was a pause. Then Jessica had an inspiration. 'I know! We'll drop them in the lake. Nobody will find them there.'

It was settled. A few days later, Mr Haggerthwaite reported that the Vortex had gone up, and the same day Robbie telephoned to say that the TV crew were coming to do their filming the following Saturday. This fitted Jessica's plans beautifully. She persuaded her parents that she and Midge should go and spend Friday night at Aunt Kate's, so that Mr and Mrs Haggerthwaite could have a night out together (something they had not had in a long while). Aunt Kate always had a long lie-in on Saturday mornings which meant that Jessica and Midge would be able to creep out undetected. The scene was set.

Chapter Six

'Anyone would think these rocks were made of plutonium!' Jessica exclaimed to Midge and Robbie. Seeing their blank faces, she explained, 'It's the densest material there is.'

'If you mean they're heavy, then say so,' Robbie snarled. 'Me, I'm beginning to think this is a fortress, not a Vortex!'

He had a point. The Vortex had not looked much at first: a column of rocks, with a path of smaller stones arranged round it in a spiral. A rather ugly column of rocks, they thought, although according to Robbie, who had it from his dad, they were a particularly rare and expensive Italian granite. But whatever they were made of, there was no doubt they were heavy. 'How many rocks did they use?'

demanded Jessica. 'It feels like a whole quarryful.'

They were all tired and bad tempered. None of them had slept well, and five o'clock was horribly early to get up on a weekend. Jessica and Robbie had immediately begun arguing about how best to dismantle the Vortex. Jessica put forward various schemes based on gravitational forces and the conservation of energy, while Robbie still wanted to blow it up – this time by using a load of fireworks which had been left over from the New Year display at the hotel. While they were arguing Midge had slipped away. When he returned he was pushing a wheelbarrow.

'I saw Dad using it last week, down by the lake,' he said, as they stared at him in admiration.

After that things went much quicker, and soon they had tipped the last load of rocks into the lake.

'She'll think it's been *spirited* away!' Jessica cackled.

'Yeah, well, I've got some sausage rolls that I spirited away from the kitchens,' said Robbie. 'Let's go and eat them.'

They were about to leave when they heard a twig snap. They glanced nervously at each other, then dived behind the nearest bush. It was a big one, fortunately. Then they held their breath and waited.

There was the sound of more twigs snapping.

Whoever was coming was not light on their feet. Then Mr Flotsam appeared. He peered around him with a very suspicious look on his face.

In their hiding place, the three conspirators hardly dared to move. Had he seen them? It seemed they were safe. A few seconds later, Mr Flotsam turned and went off towards the hotel.

'Did he notice the Vortex was gone?' whispered Jessica.

'I don't know,' said Robbie.

Jessica and Midge ran all the way back to Aunt Kate's, and had just managed to hide all their grubby gear and get themselves more or less clean by the time their aunt appeared. After breakfast they set off once again to the hotel, where they found Robbie waiting for them, halfway up a tall beech tree with a good view of the rose garden.

Soon after, the TV crew arrived. They lugged their equipment across the lawn, round the tennis courts and through the vegetable patch. They were not pleased when they found that the very object they had come to film had disappeared. But their angry voices were soon drowned out by Xandra's hysterics, Mr Flotsam's enraged bellowings and Agapanthus's tantrums when she realised that she was not going to be on television after all.

The three watchers laughed so hard they almost fell out of the tree. Their hard work had been well worth it.

Not surprisingly, Jessica felt rather sleepy that afternoon. She lay sunbathing on the lawn, listening to the birdsong, and trying to ignore the smell coming from the seaweed Mrs Haggerthwaite had hung out to dry on the branches of the apple tree. Midge was pottering about somewhere, but Jessica did not pay attention, and hardly noticed the distant sound of the front-door bell. Then she heard raised voices. She listened for a moment, then leapt up, yelled to Midge, and ran towards the house. Midge came out of the garden shed and followed her.

Xandra and Mrs Haggerthwaite were confronting one another in the kitchen.

'Sabotage!' Xandra was shouting. Her usually dreamy eyes were glittering with anger, and her wispy blonde hair was sparking out angry energy. 'I have never been so humiliated in my life! All the cameras were set up, I'd been through make-up and everything, my lines were all prepared – and – and it had completely disappeared! The Vortex was gone! What have you got to say to that?'

'That you must have looked a right ninny,' said Mrs Haggerthwaite calmly.

'And I know who's to blame! Who else would want my Vortex except you?'

'I can't imagine,' said Mrs Haggerthwaite. 'Actually I don't want it either. What would I do with a pile of rocks?'

'Very funny!' Xandra snapped. 'I know your game! You're jealous and you want to make me look ridiculous! First your daughter ruins my presentation – and I was planning to get loads of clients that way. And now this. Tell me where you were last night!'

'If it's any of your business, I was eating dinner with my husband at the Bellstone Brasserie,' replied Mrs Haggerthwaite at once. Her eyes were flashing, but she just about managed to keep her temper. 'You can phone them up and ask.'

Xandra glowered. 'And this morning?'

'I was in the garden from six o'clock this morning, hanging seaweed out to dry. I use it for my spells. I know for a fact that several people saw me – they came to complain about the smell.'

'Then you stole it during the night!'

'Don't be ridiculous.' Mrs Haggerthwaite gave an angry snort. 'But you are welcome to question the neighbours. I am sure if I *had* been creeping along the road, with a Spiritual Vortex in my sack, at three o'clock in the morning, somebody would have noticed. Bellstone is that kind of town.'

Xandra stamped her foot. 'Don't be stupid! You couldn't possibly carry it alone. It's far too heavy.'

'There you are then,' said Mrs Haggerthwaite.

This maddened Xandra even more, and soon she was ranting about how Mrs Haggerthwaite would go to any length to get rid of a competitor, and how she, Xandra, had always said that witches were a sneaky, black-hearted lot. This infuriated Mrs Haggerthwaite, who lost her temper too. In a moment, they were both bawling at each other.

Jessica exchanged a relieved glance with Midge. At least nobody suspected them. Then she felt somebody staring at her. For the first time she noticed Agapanthus, peering around her mother with accusing eyes.

Agapanthus tugged her mother's arm. 'Where were *they* last night?' she demanded, pointing at Midge and Jessica. 'I bet they did it!'

Before anyone else could say anything, Mrs Haggerthwaite spoke. 'How dare you! My children had nothing to do with this!'

'Where were they then, last night?' demanded Xandra.

'They were with their aunt,' Mrs Haggerthwaite announced. 'Miss Kate Haggerthwaite, a pillar of the community, a magistrate and winner of the best-baked scones at the Bellstone Show three years in succession! You ask her, if you don't believe me.'

Jessica had an inspiration. 'And this morning we were with Robbie Flotsam. You can ask him if you like.'

Xandra's face fell. Jessica had guessed that she

would not want to accuse Robbie of anything – not while she was busy sucking up to his father.

Mrs Haggerthwaite did not hesitate to rub it in. 'Why don't you go and tell the *Gazette* about it?' she snapped. 'Go and tell them that Robbie Flotsam has stolen his own father's Vortex! That will make a good story! It's almost as believable as all that moonshine you gave them in the story about *you*.'

Xandra went white. 'What do you mean by that?'

'I mean this!' Mrs Haggerthwaite picked up her copy of the *Bellstone Gazette* – by now rather dog-eared, and covered in tea stains and tomato ketchup – and shook it in Xandra's face. 'All this nonsense! Talk with the spirits, indeed! I expect they'd have two words to say to you! And as for this photo – what a joke! You can't fly – any more than pigs can!'

For a moment Xandra looked as if she was going to hit Mrs Haggerthwaite. Then the anger cleared and she laughed. It was a sweet, tinkly kind of laugh. Exactly the kind of laugh, in fact, that was sure to infuriate Mrs Haggerthwaite. 'You know *your* problem. You're jealous.'

'Jealous!' Mrs Haggerthwaite spluttered.

'Yes. Everyone knows witches are supposed to fly. On broomsticks, usually. Rather quaint, I've always thought.'

'You know perfectly well,' Mrs Haggerthwaite said, 'that I am not that kind of witch!'

'So, what kind of witch *are* you?' asked Xandra sweetly. 'The kind that plods to the bus stop? The kind that tramps down for her shopping in the rain? The kind that can't really do magic at all?'

Mrs Haggerthwaite was being goaded beyond endurance. 'Of course I could fly if I wanted to!' she burst out.

Jessica heard Midge groan behind her. She did not feel too happy herself. Their mother had gone too far.

'Mum—' Jessica began, but nobody paid attention.

'I don't believe you,' said Xandra, with another tinkly laugh.

'I most certainly can!'

'Show me then.' Suddenly, Xandra was not laughing any more.

'Well – I mean – not immediately—'

'Then when? Two days? Two weeks?'

Xandra was smiling now, as if she knew Mrs Haggerthwaite must back down. But if she thought that, she did not know Mrs Haggerthwaite.

'Two weeks!' Mrs Haggerthwaite pronounced. 'You'll see!'

'I can hardly wait,' murmured Xandra. She exchanged a glance with Agapanthus, and they both laughed. 'I'll see you then.' And the two of them went out of the front door together.

As soon as they had gone, Jessica turned on her mother. Mrs Haggerthwaite had suddenly become very busy fussing over Liverwort and settling him into his tank.

'Mum,' said Jessica. 'Have you gone completely nuts? You know perfectly well you can't fly.'

'I know nothing of the sort,' said Mrs Haggerthwaite, hunting around for Liverwort's food.

'No human beings can fly,' Jessica stated. 'Not by themselves. It's impossible.'

'Oh, is that right?' said Mrs Haggerthwaite. At long last, she looked up and met Jessica's eye. 'Everyone knows witches can fly. It's just that, these days, other forms of transport are generally more convenient.'

'Mum,' said Jessica slowly, 'are you seriously saying you've been travelling around on a broomstick all these years, and we just haven't noticed?'

'No,' Mrs Haggerthwaite admitted. 'I have never flown before. But that doesn't mean I couldn't if I wanted to.' And she stared at them defiantly. Her children stared back in horror.

'Go on, then,' said Jessica at last. 'Give us a demonstration.'

Mrs Haggerthwaite tossed back her long black hair. 'Of course I can't, just like that. I shall have to do some research. Look through my spellbooks.

Consult my fellow witches. But I am absolutely confident that I shall find a way. Just you wait and see.' And she swept out of the room.

Midge and Jessica looked at each other. 'This is a nightmare,' said Midge.

Jessica said nothing. There seemed to be nothing to say.

Chapter Seven

It was, the whole of her family agreed, the craziest thing that Mrs Haggerthwaite had ever done – or claimed to do. None of them had ever heard anything quite so ridiculous. 'It's utter madness!' declared Mr Haggerthwaite, when his children told him what had happened. And for the remainder of the day the three of them did their best to convince Mrs Haggerthwaite that she could not fly. They even called Aunt Kate, and she came round and argued with Mrs Haggerthwaite too.

'You'll have to back down sooner or later, Mel,' she declared roundly. 'Otherwise you'll be the laughing stock of Bellstone. That Xandra will tell everyone she meets. And if this gets into the *Gazette*—' She did not finish. She did not have to.

'I will not back down,' said Mrs Haggerthwaite between gritted teeth. 'Flying is well within my powers, I am convinced.'

'In that case, you'll not only be the laughing stock of Bellstone, but you'll also break every bone in your body,' Jessica predicted.

But the more everyone argued, the more stubborn Mrs Haggerthwaite became. Nothing would persuade her to go round to Lavender Avenue and tell 'that woman' she was withdrawing. In two weeks' time she would fly – or die in the attempt.

At this, Aunt Kate announced she was off home, declaring that she hoped Mrs Haggerthwaite had taken out a life insurance policy 'for the sake of the children'. Mrs Haggerthwaite was not impressed by this comment, and nor were Jessica and Midge. After all, as Jessica pointed out, no insurance company was going to insure somebody against something as stupid as trying to fly. So it was not as if they could look forward to any cash payments. For some reason she could not understand, this comment put Mrs Haggerthwaite in a worse mood than ever.

Dinner that evening was not a cheerful affair. Mr Haggerthwaite was so busy arguing with his wife that he burnt the casserole. At the end of the meal, Mrs Haggerthwaite rushed off to phone a fellow witch in Croydon who she was sure would know an absolutely sure-fire charm for flying, and Mr Haggerthwaite went to sulk in front of the TV. Jessica and Midge held an emergency meeting in Jessica's room.

'One good thing,' said Jessica, trying to look on the bright side. 'At least Dad hasn't had time to think about what happened at the hotel gardens. At least he doesn't know we did it.'

'Huh,' said Midge. 'I expect he'll work it out. Or

Xandra will tell him she thinks it's us. He'll be as mad as a horde of wasps.'

'Oh, rubbish. Why should Xandra tell him anything?'

'Well, if she doesn't she'll tell Mr Flotsam. And that'll be a thousand times worse. Because he'll probably tell the police!'

Jessica pointed out that Mr Flotsam would not want his own son ending up in trouble with the police, but Midge said that would not stop Mr Flotsam. He would probably bribe the police to let Robbie off, and leave the Haggerthwaites to take the blame. Jessica did not know what to say to this. The truth was it was exactly the kind of thing Mr Flotsam would do. She remembered how Mr Flotsam had almost caught them this morning. She was sure he must have suspected something, to be out so early – although Robbie said he often went out for early morning prowls, ever since a thief had made off with some valuable Japanese koi from the lily pond two years ago.

'I suppose you think this is all my fault,' said Jessica.

'It *is* all your fault,' said Midge. 'I warned you not to stir things up between Mum and Xandra.'

'I like that! The whole thing started because I was trying *not* to stir things up! A lot of good that did.

And how could I guess that getting rid of the Vortex would lead to Mum doing this?'

Jessica sighed. Only her mother could be mad enough to claim she could fly. Then she realised this was not quite true. *Agapanthus's* mother had claimed exactly the same thing – in the *Bellstone Gazette* and at Jessica's school. She had even produced a photograph which seemed to prove it. Of course, there must be some trick involved somewhere. Or was there? Could Xandra really

have found a way to fly, or at least to look as if she was? And if so, could Mrs Haggerthwaite do the same thing?

But Jessica could not think what that trick might be. And Xandra would certainly never tell her.

Midge said, 'It doesn't matter whose fault it is. The important thing is to find a way out. And I've thought of two. One: Mum backs down—'

'Mum'll never back down.'

'Which leaves Two: Mum flies.'

'That's very helpful,' said Jessica sarcastically.

'*Isn't* there some way Mum could fly?' Midge asked. Then, as Jessica stared at him in astonishment, 'I was just wondering . . . whether there might be . . . some scientific way, perhaps.'

'Of course there isn't,' said Jessica crossly. 'Not unless she was attached to a hot air balloon or something. And Xandra would be sure to say that didn't count.'

'Well, then, isn't there a *magical* way she could fly? I mean, don't you remember when you discovered that sometimes witchcraft can do things that you don't expect?'

Jessica frowned. It was true that she herself had discovered that Mrs Haggerthwaite's potions could sometimes be surprisingly effective – and for scientific reasons too. But *flying*? A potion could not make you fly, surely? 'If there really *was* a way of flying,' she said, 'wouldn't someone have found it by now?'

'But scientists haven't discovered everything, have they?'

'That's true,' Jessica admitted. 'At least, I hope they haven't. Otherwise there won't be anything left for me to discover when I'm a scientist.' Suddenly her eyes gleamed. For how would it be if she, Jessica Haggerthwaite, discovered a way for humans to fly through the air? It would be amazing! And she would be famous. In fact she would immediately become one of the most famous scientists in history!

And surely it couldn't be *impossible*, thought Jessica hopefully. After all, birds flew, insects flew. Humans were heavier than birds, of course, but pterodactyls had flown – and they must have been heavier than humans. Already, her mind was whirring. She knew there were several books about dinosaurs in the school library. And perhaps there really was something hidden away in one of Mrs Haggerthwaite's old witchcraft books. An old, forgotten method – something which, when brought under the scrutiny of Jessica's scientific mind, might lead to an amazing breakthrough!

Hah! thought Jessica suddenly. *They'll be begging me to go on their TV shows then!*

'Midge,' she said aloud, 'you may be on to something! Anyway, it's our only hope. Tomorrow, I shall start my research.'

Chapter Eight

The week that followed was a busy one for the Haggerthwaites. Both Mrs Haggerthwaite and Jessica were absorbed in their different quests for flight. For Mrs Haggerthwaite it meant poring over her spell books. Jessica typed up a new list.

AIM: Find Way for Mum to Fly
HOW: (1) investigate turbo-engines, pterodactyls, gravity, bumble bees, birds, rocket launchers, bats, hovercraft, etc
(2) sneak a look at Mum's spellbooks
(3) twist Agapanthus's arm to find out how Xandra did it.
THERE MUST BE A WAY!

Mr Haggerthwaite tried to forget about his wife's new scheme by throwing himself into his work. At least the gardens were shaping up wonderfully, he said. 'Everything's blooming, and whoever walked off with that Vortex – well, I don't condone it, but there's no denying the place looks a hundred times better without it. Mind you,' he added, 'I wouldn't be the folks that took it when Mr Flotsam catches up with them!'

Luckily he did not notice Jessica and Midge glancing at each other nervously. Nor did anyone notice that Midge was spending a lot of time in the garden shed.

By the end of the week, Jessica had discovered many interesting things. She knew, for example, more than she had ever wanted about turbo-engines and aerofoils. She had learnt that many birds have hollow bones, and that the wings of a humming-bird beat one hundred times a second. She understood the relative merits of jet engines over propellers, and knew that the bat is the only mammal that can fly. She could explain how in the physics of flight, lift is the force that takes you up, while thrust propels you forward; while gravity and drag pull you in the opposite direction. But she still did not see how any of this was going to help Mrs Haggerthwaite fly.

On the way to and from school, she tried out different ideas on Midge. On Monday, she suggested they strap Mrs Haggerthwaite to a mini-glider, made of plywood. On Tuesday, she wondered if they might attach her to a tank of kerosene and set it on fire ('Well, jet engines burn kerosene, after all'). On Wednesday, she thought if Mrs Haggerthwaite did not eat anything for the next week, she might be light enough to float downwards on the air, like a baby bird in the Amazon jungle. ('It'll take more than a week's dieting to turn her into a baby bird,' said Midge grimly.) On Thursday, she talked about pumping her full of air, like a turbo-engine; and on Friday, her idea was to fit flaps of cloth under her arms so that she could glide from tree to tree, like a cougar.

Midge was not impressed with any of these suggestions, while Jessica was beginning to have terrible dreams after reading late into the night. Dreams where Mrs Haggerthwaite came rushing through the air on huge wings, like a giant bat, or went shooting up into the stratosphere, propelled by her own personal rocket launcher.

She was beginning to have a nasty suspicion that human beings could not fly after all.

She also tried reading her mother's spellbooks (that is, when Mrs Haggerthwaite was not perusing

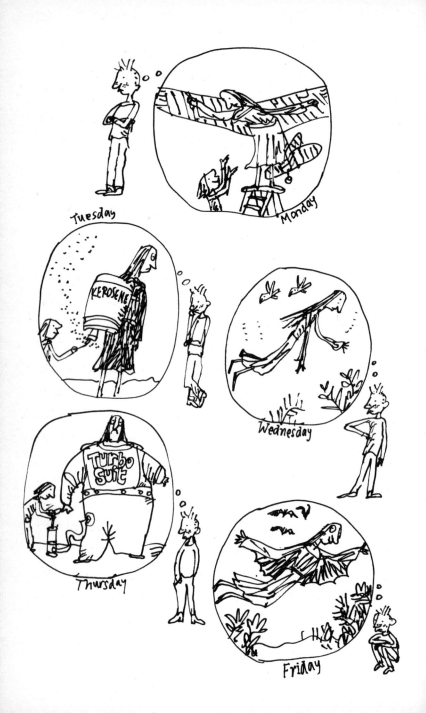

Tuesday

Monday

Wednesday

Thursday

Friday

them herself). But they were not much use either. Perhaps it was because so many of the spells were written in terrible handwriting, in green ink. But even when she could make them out, they all seemed to be for useless things like 'how to dissolve a spot or pustule on the nose' or 'how to relieve a loved one of bad breath'.

She had a feeling her mother was getting nowhere either. Mrs Haggerthwaite's calls to her fellow witches were getting more frequent and more desperate. Her family grew accustomed to tripping over her, sitting in the middle of some strange chalk diagram on the floor, chanting a new incantation, as she tried to find a way to fly.

Jessica returned to science. But, 'I don't have the right books!' she declared disgustedly. It was lunch time, and she was sitting opposite Midge in the school library with a notebook next to her and an enormous book on dinosaurs propped up in front of her. 'They're just baby's books! They don't give equations or anything!'

'Then your mum's going to look dead stupid, isn't she?' said a familiar voice, making Jessica jump. Agapanthus emerged from the history section. She came forward and pointed at a picture of a pterodactyl. 'Though that does look like your mum.' She giggled.

Jessica shut the book with a bang. 'This research is nothing to do with my mother,' she lied. 'It's – it's to do with the TV programmes I'm going to present.'

'Don't be stupid, Jessica. You don't think anybody believes you're going to be on television, do you? Even though you told everyone you were. In *public*. So you're going to look terribly stupid when you don't.'

Jessica almost hurled the pterodactyl book at her. She had almost forgotten her rash words, and was not happy to be reminded of them. Midge said, 'If Jessica says she's going to do a thing, she does it' (which was very nice and loyal of him, Jessica thought, except that she had no idea how she was going to live up to his words). Still, at the sight of Agapanthus's disbelieving sneer, she felt some of her old determination welling up.

'I am putting it in hand this very afternoon,' she announced grandly.

'I'll believe it when I see it,' sneered Agapanthus.

She turned to leave but Jessica said quickly, in what she hoped was a casual voice, 'It must have been wonderful for you, watching your mum fly.'

'Yes, it would have been – I mean, it was, yes,' said Agapanthus, taken by surprise. She made for the door, but Jessica grabbed her arm.

'You've never seen her fly, have you?'

Agapanthus blushed. 'Mum likes to be alone, when the Spirits levitate her.'

'Is that so? Then who took the photo for the *Bellstone Gazette*?'

Agapanthus wrenched her arm away. 'You don't

understand anything!' she snapped, and ran away before Jessica could stop her.

'Hmmm,' said Jessica thoughtfully.

Jessica had almost forgotten about her TV ambitions, she had been so busy researching flight. But now, spurred into action by Agapanthus, she realised that the time had come. At the end of school she went up to Robbie and told him, 'I'm coming home with you. I need to speak to your dad.'

Robbie was alarmed. 'Why do you want to see him? I think we should keep out of his way. He's really fed up about his Spiritual Vortex disappearing, and he keeps wondering who took it.'

'I can't help that.' Jessica spotted Midge across the playground. 'Midge!' she yelled. 'D'you want to come to the hotel?'

Midge said he did, and as they walked along the two boys tried to work out exactly what Jessica was up to. But she would reveal nothing.

'Do you believe determination can accomplish anything?' she asked, changing the subject.

'What, anything?' asked Robbie, blinking.

'Yes. Do you believe, that as long as you try hard enough, there is always *a way*?'

'How d'you mean, *a way*?'

'A way to succeed, of course! To get what you want from life!'

Robbie scratched his head. He was not used to these kinds of questions. 'Err – I dunno. I suppose so. If you try hard enough. My dad's got something like that written up on the wall, in his office. In a gold frame.'

'Huh,' said Jessica. 'Then it's sure to be wrong.'

'If at first you don't succeed, try, try again,' said Midge. 'That's what they say. D'you mean a way for Mum to fly? Haven't you found one yet? You've got to keep trying!'

'Yeah, well,' said Robbie. 'There are ways and then there are miracles. Still,' he added, 'if anybody can find a way, you can, Jessie.'

Jessica sighed. She was so despondent that she didn't even tell him off for calling her Jessie. 'I just wish I believed you!'

Still, she seemed her old self as she marched into Mr Flotsam's office, with Robbie and Midge trailing behind. Mr Flotsam was sitting at his huge, mahogany desk, checking through some papers. The gold-framed motto that Robbie had mentioned – *Determination Breeds Success: Success Breeds Money!* – hung on the wall behind him.

'Ah! It's little Jessica,' he boomed, in a jovial way. 'I haven't seen you in ages.'

Jessica scowled. 'I've been busy,' she said abruptly.

'You're always busy, you Haggerthwaites,' said Mr Flotsam. 'Still, I can't complain. Your dad is doing a marvellous job of the garden. It's going to look magnificent. Pity our Vortex got pinched though.' Suddenly, he looked mean and brooding. Robbie shifted uncomfortably beside Jessica. 'I wonder what happened to it,' pondered Mr Flotsam. 'Just wait until I catch the people responsible!'

'Yes, well, what I was wondering about,' said Jessica quickly, 'is this friend of yours. The one who makes TV programmes. I need to meet him.'

'Ah, fancy going on TV, do you, Jessica?' Mr Flotsam chuckled as if he found this a good joke.

'Yes, I do, actually,' said Jessica.

'Well, well,' said Mr Flotsam, once he had managed to stop laughing. 'You're a little girl who knows what she wants! But you can't just march into a TV studio and expect them to sign you up. Even if there was a TV studio in Bellstone – which there isn't. No, you have to find a quiet moment, take them for a drink, flatter them a little.'

'Oh,' said Jessica. This sounded more difficult than she had anticipated. But she lifted her chin. 'I don't care,' she said firmly. 'I'll get Mum or Dad to drive me to the studio. And then I'll make them listen to me!'

'Hmm,' said Mr Flotsam. 'Determination. That's what I like to see. I'll tell you what. I'll give my friend Bill a call now and see if he can come over. I wouldn't mind a word with him myself.'

Jessica was amazed – it was almost too easy! She wondered why she had wasted so much time writing letters and making phone calls. She actually felt grateful to Mr Flotsam – which was rather

uncomfortable, because it made her feel guilty for disliking him so much. Luckily her gratitude began to fade as she listened to Mr Flotsam's end of the conversation.

'Most amusing young miss,' Mr Flotsam boomed, 'knows her own mind. She'll give you a laugh if nothing else.' Then Mr Flotsam put down the phone and announced, 'He'll be here in an hour to see you. Now, what would you young folks like to do in the meantime? I expect you'd like a free tea in the hotel restaurant, wouldn't you?'

They had to admit they would. So he took them downstairs himself, settled them at a table with a lace tablecloth, and told the head waiter that they were to have as many sandwiches and cakes as they liked. Jessica began to feel grateful and guilty all over again.

By her third éclair (bursting with chocolate and cream) Jessica decided that Mr Flotsam was one of the nicest people she knew. When they could eat no more they sat licking their sticky fingers and (in Jessica and Midge's case) hoping that Mr Haggerthwaite would not be making anything too heavy for supper.

'That was fantastic,' said Midge happily. 'The meringues were even better than Aunt Kate's.' Then his expression changed.

'What's the matter?' asked Robbie. 'Eaten too much?'

'I just remembered something,' said Midge. 'I forgot to feed – to feed Liverwort. I'd better go.' And he leapt up.

'Don't worry,' Jessica called after him. 'Mum will feed him.' But Midge was already out of the door. Jessica frowned. 'He's been acting very strangely lately,' she said to Robbie. 'He keeps disappearing. And he's started taking Liverwort to school again. After all the trouble it caused!'

But before he could reply, a man entered the room and strode up to their table. 'You must be Jessica,' he said. 'I'm Bill Mycroft.'

'Hello.' Jessica looked at him in surprise. As Bill Mycroft was a friend of Mr Flotsam's, she had expected him to look like Mr Flotsam: stout, balding and dressed in a business suit. But Bill Mycroft was young and lean, with streaks in his hair and designer jeans. He also seemed in an enormous rush.

'Right!' he said, grabbing a chair. 'Let's hear your pitch.'

'My pitch?' Jessica stared at him. She wondered if he meant the pitch of her voice. Perhaps that was important for television. She hoped he didn't want her to sing – not in the middle of the hotel dining room.

'Your pitch!' repeated Bill Mycroft. 'Your idea, your plan, your scheme, your project! Why it's good, why it's hot, why it's cool, why it's happening! And why I should take it up!'

'Oh, err, right.' For once Jessica was almost at a loss for words. 'Well, I just think there should be more programmes for kids about science, really,' she said weakly. Bill Mycroft did not look very impressed – but before he could say anything, Jessica pulled herself together and began to tell him all about her ideas for the first programme: Why the Dinosaurs Became Extinct. As she talked, her usual confidence came flooding back, and she could tell from the expression on Robbie's face, as he

grinned at her encouragingly, that she was doing a good job.

'So, you see, Mr Mycroft,' she finished—

'Call me Bill.'

'So, you see, Bill, I'm sure it will be a big success.'

But Bill Mycroft was shaking his head. 'You're a very intelligent young lady,' he announced, 'I can see that. And you have presence too, I don't deny it. You'd be great on TV.'

'Then what's the problem?' asked Jessica, for it was clear that there was one.

'It's the concept,' Bill explained. 'Science! Science is boring. Even dinosaurs – unless you're going to show computer animations of them eating each other and goring each other to death.' Robbie looked suddenly alert and hopeful, but Bill was shaking his head. 'And we haven't got the budget for that.'

'But I know lots of kids who like science,' said Jessica desperately.

'Oh no. They can't stand it. Unless you're talking big bucks sci-fi movies, with lots of laser-fights –'

'Great!' agreed Robbie. Jessica glared at him.

'– then kids find science boring. Magic! That's what they like these days. Particularly since Harry Potter, you know – they've all been mad for magic!'

'Well, I think you're wrong,' said Jessica. 'Just because they like magic doesn't mean they don't like science too. *Robbie's* really interested in science, aren't you, Robbie?'

'Huh?' said Robbie. Jessica kicked him under the table. 'Oh – yeah – I just love it.'

'I'm not convinced. Now if you'd offered me something to do with magic – or wizards – or witchcraft—'

'Oh, really!' Jessica lost patience. 'I'll tell you this: reading about it is one thing, but most kids would think again if they knew what it was really like, having a witch around! My mum's a witch, and let me tell you – it's no fun at all!'

Bill was staring at her with sudden attention.

'What! Do you really have a mother who's a witch?'

'I do at the moment,' said Jessica grimly. 'Only she's just decided she can fly, so this time next week I probably won't.'

'But that's amazing!' Bill was about to go on, but at that moment Mr Flotsam came bustling up to join them.

'Ah, there you are, Bill! Let me order you a drink. So you've met the young people – full of ideas, aren't they! But what I was thinking was – why don't we go and discuss all this outside. It's such a beautiful afternoon. And the gardens look fantastic, as I'm sure you will agree. In fact, I was thinking, even though we seem to have – err – mislaid our Vortex, I really don't see why that should stop you making a TV programme about them.'

Bill laughed and laughed. 'Isn't that just like you, Bert!' he said, when he had recovered. 'I might have known you were up to something. Asking me round here to meet this little girl! Of course you had another motive. I should have guessed it was all about getting your hotel on the telly.'

Jessica and Robbie glared accusingly at Mr Flotsam. Jessica wasn't feeling too fond of Bill, either (she hated being described as a little girl) but she was angrier with Mr Flotsam – all the more so because she had been feeling guilty for misjudging him. But Mr Flotsam did not even look embarrassed.

'Well, there's no harm, is there?' he said good-temperedly. 'And the fact is my gardens would look superb on the telly. And what it would do for business—'

'No, Bert. I've already told you. There's too many programmes about gardens. The market's saturated. That Vortex – all that stuff about the Spirits – it would have been a new angle, something different. Without it, we're just talking pretty flowers, and we've seen that before.'

'Of course, it is a shame about that Vortex,' Mr Flotsam admitted. 'Cost me an arm and a leg, it did. When I catch those responsible—' Suddenly, he looked at Robbie and Jessica. 'I don't suppose you two know anything about it, do you?'

Robbie and Jessica shrugged and tried to look as innocent and puzzled as possible. 'Why should we?' asked Jessica.

'Humph!' Mr Flotsam's eyes were narrowed in a way that Jessica did not much like.

'But anyway, Bert, you take my point,' interrupted Bill, who was not very interested in who had pinched Mr Flotsam's Vortex. 'There's no new angle.'

'But Tom Haggerthwaite is an absolutely brilliant

garden designer!' protested Mr Flotsam. 'You can do a whole programme about how he is transforming this place beyond recognition!'

'Yes, but who's heard of him? Now, this stuff Jessica was telling me about sounds a lot more exciting. A mother who thinks she can fly! That's

something new! When is she going to try it?'

Jessica stared at him in sudden alarm. She had not thought of this! 'But it isn't exciting at all!' she protested. She looked around the table and *knew* things were going wrong. Bill Mycroft had an eager, intent, ferocious expression on his face – the kind of expression a weasel might have on happening upon a plump young rabbit. As for Mr Flotsam – clearly he was thinking, hard. Then his face cracked into a beam. And that was worse. For there was only one thing that made Mr Flotsam beam – and that was when he had worked out how something could be made to benefit Mr Flotsam.

'I've got it!' he cried. 'She must make her attempt here! In the hotel gardens! There's lots of big trees for her to jump off – I mean fly from – and the gardens will provide the perfect backdrop. It's just the angle you need. It will be terrific TV!'

'Fantastic,' declared Bill Mycroft.

'Oh no!' cried Jessica.

Why was it, she wondered, that however carefully she planned, things always seemed to work out in the opposite way to how she had intended? And how on earth would she – and Mrs Haggerthwaite – get out of this one?

Chapter Nine

Mr Flotsam drove Jessica home in his Jaguar. Jessica was not especially grateful, as she knew he was only doing it because he wanted to tell Mrs Haggerthwaite about the TV filming. She said very little, while Mr Flotsam, who was in a very good mood indeed, chatted on about how grateful he was to Jessica for bringing the whole thing about. 'A young lady with initiative, that's what I like to see,' he thundered cheerfully, as he turned into the Haggerthwaites' street. 'Just the friend for Robbie. Speaking of which, is there any chance you could have a word with him?'

'What about?' Jessica asked suspiciously.

'Well, his behaviour, basically. Don't know if he's told you I've been seeing a bit of Xandra – you know – strange ideas, but a charming woman. But Robbie doesn't see it that way. He's been extremely rude to her.'

'Actually,' said Jessica, as they stopped outside her house, 'I think Robbie knows better than you do. That Xandra's a very shady character.'

'What do you mean by that?'

'I mean she's a liar and a cheat.' And quickly Jessica related the tale of the school presentation and the tape recorder. 'And another thing,' she went on. 'She *says* she can fly, but even *her own daughter* has never seen her do it. And yet there's a photo of her doing it in your newspaper. That seems fishy to me.'

She had been undoing her seat belt, but now she turned around to find Mr Flotsam looking so ferocious that she quickly opened the door and climbed out. 'Thanks for the lift, Mr Flotsam,' she said, and ran inside to look for Midge.

She found him in the kitchen with a tin of sardines.

'What are you doing with that?' she demanded and, not waiting for an answer, added, 'Come on – quick – it's important.' They arrived in the hall just as Mr Flotsam broke the news of her media appearance to their mother.

'Yes, they're hoping to make a whole programme

about it,' he concluded. 'Lisa Singh will interview you. She's their top young presenter you know.'

Mrs Haggerthwaite, for once, had nothing to say. She just gaped at him.

'Mum,' Jessica burst out. 'You can't possibly go on TV!'

Midge groaned. He knew that telling Mrs Haggerthwaite she could not do something was the absolute most sure-fire way to make her do it. Unfortunately, Mr Flotsam realised this too.

'Of course, if you're not up to it—' he began cunningly.

Sure enough Mrs Haggerthwaite's face was already taking on its most stubborn expression. 'There's no question of that!' she snapped. 'I'll do it! I don't care how many cameras there are!'

'And your husband?' asked Mr Flotsam, a bit surprised that she had agreed so quickly. 'What will he think?'

'He will be delighted!' Mrs Haggerthwaite lied. She avoided Jessica and Midge's eyes. 'He supports me in my ventures as I do him in his. Although,' she added, 'I may not mention it to him just yet.'

Mr Flotsam left soon after this, telling Mrs Haggerthwaite that he would be in touch. Jessica and Midge tried to persuade Mrs Haggerthwaite to change her mind but she would not listen to them. At

last she stormed off, slamming the door behind her.

'Isn't that just typical!' declared Jessica, but when she turned round, Midge had gone.

Jessica frowned. Midge really was acting very oddly. She had thought everything was all right since he had been reassured that Mr and Mrs Haggerthwaite would not split up. But now she began to wonder. He kept disappearing at strange moments. He had been taking Liverwort to school again. And what had he been doing with that tin of sardines?

She searched the house but she could not find him anywhere. At last she went into the garden, taking Liverwort with her to enjoy some fresh air. She was about to put Liverwort down on the patio, where he liked to hunt for insects, when she heard strange sounds from Mr Haggerthwaite's garden shed. Still holding Liverwort, she went and flung open the door.

'Watch out!' squawked Midge. 'He'll get away!'

Jessica leapt back as a large, white bird came towards her across the floor of the shed. It was thrusting out its head and crying 'Cark!' and snapping its beak in a far from friendly manner.

It was making for the open door. After the briefest hesitation, Jessica stepped forward into the shed, slamming the door shut behind her. The bird retreated into one corner, carking furiously. Midge made soothing noises and gave it a sardine from the can.

'What's going on?' Jessica hissed. 'That thing almost took my hand off!'

'He's not a thing! He's Archie. Isn't he lovely?'

'*Lovely!*'

The bird, having gobbled up its sardine, was now beadily eyeing Jessica. Suddenly, it lunged forward, hooking its beak towards Jessica's hand. Just in time, Jessica leapt sideways, clutching Liverwort to her chest. She had forgotten she was holding Liverwort – and that, to a large bird, he might appear an appetising snack.

'How dare you bring Liverwort in here!' yelled Midge. 'It's not safe!'

'How was I to know you had filled the shed with dangerous predators!' Jessica snapped.

'Archie is not a dangerous predator!'

'Yes he is. What is he, anyway? An eagle?'

'He's a herring gull. Don't you think he's beautiful?'

Jessica considered Archie as closely as she was able, given the darkness of the shed. He was a rather magnificent bird, she had to admit. He was covered in white feathers, his eyes were clear and bright, and his head was high and proud. 'I'd like him better if he didn't have such a large beak,' she said at last.

Midge said, 'I tell you what, let's take him into the garden. He gets a bit fed up in here. And if there's two of us we can always catch him.' He paused. 'Or d'you think a cat might get him?'

'I think I'd be more worried about the cat,' said Jessica. But Midge had already opened the shed door and was gently shooing Archie outside. 'Won't he fly away?' Jessica asked. She could not help feeling it would be no bad thing if he did.

'He can't,' Midge explained. 'He's hurt his wing.'

Sure enough, although Archie had opened his wings, and was flexing them at full length, he could not get off the ground. One of the wings dragged slightly.

'He's almost better,' said Midge. 'I think he'll be able to fly soon. I found him down in the Wilderness Garden, near the lake. He couldn't fly, so Robbie helped me get him into a crate and I brought him back here. You don't know how hard it was catching him,' he added proudly.

'Does Dad know you've got a large gull living in his shed?'

'Yes,' said Midge. 'But he said not to tell Mum. He said she had enough on her mind. And I thought you had enough on *your* mind too. Though Dad doesn't know how big Archie's got. He was only little when I found him.' As if to prove this was no longer the case, there was sudden flurry and a squawk; a squirrel had ventured into the garden and been lucky to escape with its life. Archie snapped his beak disappointedly.

'So, that's why you've been taking Liverwort to school again,' said Jessica. 'So he won't get eaten. Still, never mind that. What shall we do about Mum?'

'You mean now she's going to throw herself into Mr Flotsam's lily pond in front of a load of TV cameras?' asked Midge – which was not quite the way Jessica would have put it. 'This is your fault, Jessica.'

'That's not fair!' said Jessica.

'Yes, it is. If you hadn't made Mr Flotsam call that TV man this would never have happened. You're obsessed with getting on the telly!'

'Yes,' snapped Jessica, 'and that was your idea in the first place!'

'Hmm.' Midge could not think of a comeback.

'It seems like everyone's going on telly except me,' Jessica complained.

Midge ignored this. 'Anyway, it's more important than ever now that you find some way for Mum to fly. You can do it if you really try. I know you can.'

Jessica said nothing. She did not want to admit it to Midge, but she was losing hope. She watched Archie, as he unfurled his powerful wings and, with feathers and muscles rippling, attempted to lift off into the air. Two thoughts were forming in her mind. One was how much Archie looked like a creature of the sky, and how he would soon launch himself into his natural element. She could already picture him swooping and soaring above. Unfortunately, the other thought was that she could not picture Mrs Haggerthwaite swooping and soaring at all.

Later that evening Jessica put some fresh paper into her typewriter.

```
PROGRESS REPORT

AIM 1: To be a TV Star
Progress: None! Made contact with TV
producer today — WORSE than useless.
Says science is boring and plans to
film Mum trying to fly instead. This
is terrible news. Mum will break
every bone in her body, and the whole
world will see it.

AIM 2: Revenge on Xandra
We got rid of her rotten old Vortex
all right. So she didn't get to go on
telly (again). But I think Mr Flotsam
suspects it was us. This is BAD. I
just hope he doesn't go to the
police.
```

When Jessica had finished, she felt depressed. At least the V key on the typewriter was working again, but in the circumstances that was not much comfort. Usually, she found she could think more clearly if she wrote something down on paper – and certainly that was what *How to Get What You Want in Three Easy Stages* had suggested. But this time she could see no answers at all. She sighed, then typed a final sentence.

IT'S ALL A HORRIBLE MESS!

For various reasons, none of the family mentioned the news about Mrs Haggerthwaite's television appearance to Mr Haggerthwaite. Midge did not mention it because he was hoping that, if nobody argued with her, Mrs Haggerthwaite would finally see sense and give up the idea. Mrs Haggerthwaite did not tell him precisely because he was sure to argue with her, and she did not want to give up the idea! As for Jessica, she was secretly hoping that something would happen to make the TV company or Mr Flotsam lose interest altogether.

It didn't. A couple of days before the filming was due to take place, Jessica went over to the hotel with Midge and found Mr Flotsam standing in the middle of the lawn. He was waving his arms about and shouting through a loud-hailer at a group of burly men who were struggling back and forth with a load of scaffolding. 'Ah, Jessica, Midge!' he bellowed. 'What do you think of my tower?'

'Your tower?' repeated Jessica, staring at him.

'Yes – that's what they're building. It's for your mother to fly from, you know. We'll all get a marvellous view!'

They both gaped at him, horrified. At last Midge said, 'Does Mum know about this?'

'Of course she does! I phoned up and told her all about it. Said I wouldn't be in her shoes for a million pounds. She got really huffy with me – told me if she said she was going to do a thing, she did it – said she'd fly off the Eiffel Tower, if necessary. A woman of spirit, your mother! That's what I like about you Haggerthwaite girls – plenty of spirit.'

'Huh,' said Jessica, not pleased. 'And does *Dad* know about this?'

Mr Flotsam's face dimmed. 'Hmm, well, yes. Actually, he's not too happy. First he said all this

scaffolding would ruin his lawn. Then, when he heard what it was for – well, he really hit the roof. Threatened to quit, would you believe. But never mind that. I'm not going to let them put the scaffolding on the lawn, after all – I'm getting them to carry it down to that wild bit, next to the lake. It can't do any damage there. No, I'm sure your dad will come round. I mean, think how much publicity he'll be getting!'

Jessica thought this was typical of Mr Flotsam. Of course he *would* think Mr Haggerthwaite would be delighted to get publicity for his business – even if it meant his wife ending up in hospital, up to her neck in plaster. But Jessica knew better.

And, in fact, when they found Mr Haggerthwaite down by the rose garden he was in a terrible mood. 'You've heard have you?' he greeted them. 'About this tomfoolery? Really, I don't know who's worse. Your mother, with her madfool ideas, or Bert Flotsam, trying to cash in on them. I've told him straight – I'll hand in my notice! As for this TV crew – I don't know how they got involved!' Jessica looked at her feet and said nothing, and Mr Haggerthwaite continued, 'Enough is enough! Your mother will have to listen to sense, for once in her life. It's time for me to put my foot down!'

Suddenly, he cast his spade to one side. 'Come on.
Let's go and sort this thing out now.'

Delighted, Jessica and Midge followed him,
wondering if he really was going to settle
everything. Arriving home, Mr Haggerthwaite
strode straight through the hall and flung open the
living-room door, even though he was usually

careful not to interrupt Mrs Haggerthwaite's consultations. But there was nobody there.

'That's funny,' said Mr Haggerthwaite, his brow creasing. 'Maybe she's in the kitchen.'

But they could not find Mrs Haggerthwaite anywhere in the house. 'Maybe she's popped out to the shops,' said Midge. 'Or perhaps she's down by the canal, gathering herbs.'

'Yes, well – she'll be in for a surprise when she gets back,' said Mr Haggerthwaite.

Meanwhile, he went to put the kettle on, and Midge said he was going to check on Archie. It was Jessica who spotted a piece of paper lying on the kitchen table. 'What's this?' she said.

- FAX -
To: Mellandra Haggerthwaite,
Bellstone Witch-in-Residence
From: The High Witch of Milton Keynes

Dear Mel,
I've never tried flying but here's an incantation my Auntie Meggsy gave me for making the dead Fly by Night. Maybe it will work for the living, too. Use the Raising of the Dead magical powder (recipe attached) and scatter around. Then chant as follows: ARAMANCHA BELISHA ASCENDA…

Jessica and Mr Haggerthwaite read no further, for at that moment they heard a cry of alarm from Midge. As he had opened the door to the garden, something had stopped him in his tracks.

Jessica and Mr Haggerthwaite rushed to join him. A dreadful sight met their eyes.

Mrs Haggerthwaite was clinging to the top-most branches of the apple tree where the branches were thin and weak. She was swaying back and forth, and looked in danger of falling at any moment. Wearing her best cloak covered in magic runes, which she wore only for her most difficult spells, she scattered purple powder on the ground below.

As they watched, horrified, she began to chant, 'Aramancha Belisha Ascenda—'

'Melly!' yelled Mr Haggerthwaite. 'STOP!' And he rushed forward, his arms outstretched, just as Mrs Haggerthwaite launched herself from the tree.

But to everybody's amazement, Mrs Haggerthwaite did not plummet to the ground. Instead, she remained suspended in midair. 'I'm flying!' she shrieked happily.

Jessica and Midge gasped. Was it true? Was their mother's witchcraft really enabling her to fly?

Then the branch on which Mrs Haggerthwaite's

cloak had caught itself gave way. With a terrible shriek, she fell . . .

Jessica and Midge went racing forwards to discover what, if anything, of their parents remained.

As Jessica told her parents sternly some time later, in the Accident and Emergency Department of Bellstone General Hospital, it was a wonder they had not both been killed. Aunt Kate agreed. Jessica had telephoned Aunt Kate as soon as she had worked out that her parents were still alive (although both groaning horribly) and Aunt Kate had rushed round with her First Aid Kit. Then, when she had realised this was not sufficient, she had driven them all to the hospital. And she had plenty to say about 'foolishness' and 'people needing their heads examining' and 'should be old enough to know better'.

'Don't carry on, Kate,' said Mr Haggerthwaite. 'I've got six stitches in my forehead, and a cracking headache.'

'Yes, and it wasn't Dad's fault,' said Midge. 'Dad probably saved Mum's life.'

Everybody turned to look at Mrs Haggerthwaite. She had a broken arm all done up in plaster, a leg in plaster too, and a big bruise on her cheek. She had

already been told she would have to stay in hospital
for a couple of days. She was drinking a cup of tea
one handed and (most unusually for her) being
extremely quiet.

'Well, what do you want me to say?' she
demanded, with a show of her old spirit. Then
she drooped, and stared down into her cup,
looking like a puppy that knows it has done
wrong. 'It was my fault,' she said in a small voice.
'I'm sorry.'

'Never mind that,' said Mr Haggerthwaite. 'I
want your solemn promise that you will give up this

flying lark once and for all. Why, I thought you were going to be killed!'

'But everybody will laugh at me!' bleated Mrs Haggerthwaite. 'Everybody will know that I backed down!'

'I don't care,' said Mr Haggerthwaite. 'At least you will be in one piece. Almost,' he added.

'Anyway,' Jessica pointed out, 'I don't see how you *can* fly now. Even with magic. You've only one arm to flap, or one hand to hold on to a broomstick.'

'That's true,' said Mrs Haggerthwaite. She sighed. 'All right. I promise.'

Mr Haggerthwaite gave a sigh of relief.

'But what will happen now?' his wife went on. 'I'll have to tell Mr Flotsam. And he'll probably put it in the *Gazette*! And I'd better get on to the TV company and – oh, I hate backing down!'

There was a rushing noise in Jessica's head, as if everything was spinning around . . . then settling in a new order. 'Don't worry,' said Jessica. 'I'll look after everything.' She grinned. 'I've had an idea.'

Chapter Ten

It was rather nice, in some ways, having Mrs Haggerthwaite in hospital. No funny smells wafting around the house from her potions. No feeling something slimy on your neck and realising you had walked into some seaweed, hanging out to dry. No taking an ice-cold jug of lemonade from the fridge, and discovering it contained pondwater needed for one of her spells (or sometimes something *worse*). Furthermore, Mr Haggerthwaite was in such a good mood, now that he knew that Mrs Haggerthwaite was safe, that he let Jessica and Midge have chips with every meal, and he even let Midge bring Archie inside the house to watch TV. Still, the place did seem very quiet without her, and when Saturday morning dawned, and Jessica tiptoed through a silent house and almost slipped and fell on a pile of seagull droppings, she found she was looking forward to her mother coming home after all.

But first, there were other things to do. Today was the day that Mrs Haggerthwaite was *supposed* to be going to fly. Jessica felt it was up to her to save Mrs Haggerthwaite's reputation as a professional witch. And Jessica had to think of her own reputation too.

Jessica had hoped she would get to the Wilderness Garden before anybody else. But there was already quite a crowd when she arrived. The camera crew from Mind-Boggling TV were there and were busy setting up cameras and sound equipment near the lake. A big platform had been built there, with a red carpet and lots of ribbons and flowers. In the middle of it was the scaffolding tower from which Mrs Haggerthwaite was supposed to fly. There was a staircase with another red carpet leading up to it. At the back of the platform, a group of Mr Flotsam's hotel workers were setting up a big banner. It read:

Human Flight – A First for Bellstone and the World!
Brought to you by Flotsam's Luxury Hotels
Number One Choice for the Discerning Traveller.

Meanwhile, Mr Flotsam was puffing here and

there, giving orders and trying to make sure that as much of his gardens as possible would be included in the TV footage.

Undaunted by the bustle, Jessica swung herself up onto the platform, and went to check out the terrain. She knew this was vital if her scheme was going to succeed.

When Robbie and Midge arrived a little later, they could not see her anywhere.

'Where's she got to?' Robbie asked Midge, having found him at the fallen log next to the lake. 'I thought she was coming with you.'

'No, she left the house before breakfast,' Midge explained. 'But she'll be all right. Have you got any sardines?'

Robbie stared at him as if he was mad. 'Sardines? Why should I have sardines?' Then his eyes fell on the crate nearby. 'Oh – I see. I expect we can nick some from the hotel kitchens, if you like.'

Their mission soon accomplished (Robbie was an old hand at raiding the hotel kitchens), they sat beneath a tree and munched on some crisps they had found in the same cupboard as the sardines. Meanwhile, Midge filled Robbie in on as much of Jessica's plans as he had been told – which wasn't much.

'She wouldn't tell me everything,' said Midge. 'She wouldn't tell Dad, even.'

'And all she would tell me, on the phone, was to meet her at the fallen log. And then she wasn't there,' grumbled Robbie.

'I heard that! And I am here!' Jessica appeared from behind a tree, looking extremely cheerful, and not at all apologetic for being late.

'What's going on?' Robbie demanded. 'And don't tell me your mum's going to fly. I'm not stupid.'

Jessica and Midge ignored this last comment. They had agreed to keep secret Mrs Haggerthwaite's disastrous attempt at flight. Jessica said, 'There isn't time to explain. But listen. You're good with ropes – aren't you?'

Robbie stared at her as if she had gone mad. 'What did you have in mind?' he asked. 'Climbing them? Tying people up? Lassooing somebody?' He thought about it, then admitted, 'Actually, I am quite good at all of those.'

'It's more a matter of *untying* really,' Jessica said. She quickly explained what she wanted him to do. 'And that platform is placed just right,' she concluded. 'It's perfect! As long as you do your bit.'

'Oh, Midge and me will sort that out.'

'Good. And Midge – did you bring him?' Midge indicated the box, from which snapping sounds were coming.

'Great. Now, Robbie will help you carry him.'

'I wish someone would tell me what's going on,' Robbie complained.

'There's no time! They're starting soon. I have to look for your dad.' She gave them her last instructions, then ran off, leaving Robbie staring after her.

A large crowd had gathered by now, including photographers from the *Bellstone Gazette*, guests from the hotel, and a number of people from the town who had heard something was going on. There were plenty of people from school, including

Clare, and even Sam Harris, whose mother was terribly fussy and seldom let him go anywhere outside his own back garden. He spotted Robbie and came over.

'Hi, Robbie,' he said shyly. 'How about a kick around?'

'Nah,' said Robbie, a little surprised (for Sam was a timid boy, and timid boys usually avoided Robbie Flotsam). Then he thought for a moment. 'How are you with reef knots?'

Meanwhile, Jessica was searching the crowds for Mr Flotsam. She eventually spotted him standing next to a refreshment stall manned by waiters from his hotel. He was looking very pleased with himself, which was not surprising. Judging from the long lines of people waiting, and the sky-high prices, he was going to do very well indeed.

'Hello, Mr Flotsam,' said Jessica.

'Ah, Jessica! Have some lemonade. And some cake.' He took a complacent look at the lines of customers. 'Have it on me!'

'Mr Flotsam,' said Jessica, ignoring this, 'I've been talking to the TV people, and to Mum. They asked me to come and tell you what's been decided about the filming.'

Mr Flotsam's eyes narrowed. 'What's that? What *they've* decided! They should have asked *me* first!'

'I know,' said Jessica solemnly. 'But we all knew you would say you wanted to keep to the background, because that's the kind of modest person you are. But actually it's terribly important that you should be the one to make the introductions at the start.'

As she had hoped, Mr Flotsam fell for this at once – which was a good thing, as Jessica had not, in fact, spoken with the TV people at all. Luckily, Mr Flotsam was so flattered at being asked to appear,

that he listened like a complete lamb while Jessica explained what she wanted him to do.

When she had finished, he nodded. 'That all sounds very satisfactory. But if I am to make the introductions –' he began to preen himself – 'I had better go into make-up now. Image is all important in business, you know!' He disappeared. A few moments later Jessica spotted one of the TV make-up girls attacking his bald patch with a powder puff.

'So that's settled!' Jessica made her way through the crowd, this time in search of Bill Mycroft. He was standing near Lisa Singh, Mind-Boggling TV's well-known children's TV presenter.

'Oh, there you are, Jessica,' said Bill. 'Enjoying yourself? I expect you want Lisa's autograph?'

Jessica took a deep breath. 'I've been talking to Mr Flotsam and Mum,' she announced. 'And they asked me to come and tell you what's been decided.'

Bill Mycroft frowned slightly. 'It's not for them to tell us—'

Jessica interrupted. 'But it's really great TV! It's really – *hot* and, err – *happening*!' And before he could protest, she rushed into an explanation.

Luckily, he made no more objections. 'I suppose there's no reason why old Bert shouldn't make the introductions if he wants to,' he said, when she had finished. 'And if you want to stand on the platform – that's OK too.'

Jessica hurried away because she had spotted Mr Haggerthwaite, looking unusually smart in a shirt and tie, just in case some of the media present might want to interview him about the gardens. He was also looking extremely worried. 'I didn't think there would be so many people here!' he told her. 'What will happen to your mum? I don't want her to get hurt. After all, she's not in the best of health.'

'She'll be fine.'

'I hope so.' Mr Haggerthwaite shook his head. 'I don't know why I agreed to this.'

'But she is coming, isn't she?'

'Yes, just as you arranged.' He looked at her with a thoughtful expression, then said, 'You're good at arranging things, Jessica. I've been wondering – I don't suppose you arranged for that Spiritual Vortex to disappear, did you?'

Jessica went crimson. She did not know what to say. To her relief Mr Haggerthwaite suddenly grinned.

'Well, we'll say no more about it, this time. But if this should ever happen again—'

'Dad,' said Jessica fervently, 'I promise you, I will never take another Spiritual Vortex!'

'See that you don't.' He winked. 'Good luck. Not that you need it. You'll be great!' And he left.

Jessica laughed. She felt hugely relieved. And then, suddenly, she felt very strange indeed. Her dad had confidence in her – yet she was suddenly full of doubt. Had she taken on too much? Was she going to let her family and Robbie down? Worse still, was she about to make a complete fool of herself in front of everybody? She began to wonder if it was too late to call the whole thing off.

Her knees had gone all weak and trembly, so she sat down on the platform, half-listening to the piece that Lisa Singh was recording to camera, nearby.

'Hi, viewers, I'm Lisa Singh, and do we have a fantastic, whizz-bang programme lined up for you today! In just a moment Mellandra Haggerthwaite, Britain's top professional witch, is going to be using her famed magical powers in an attempt to fly – that's right, fly – and we'll be here, bringing you every thrilling second . . .'

Jessica spotted two familiar people, approaching her across the grass. She took a deep breath. Then she got to her feet.

'Well, hello, Jessica,' cooed Xandra. She and Agapanthus were wearing beautiful, matching tunics, their hair arranged in elaborate, flowing ringlets. 'Your mother has drawn quite a crowd.'

'Well, she is well known in Bellstone,' said Jessica.

'Pity they're about to see her fall on her head,'

said Agapanthus. 'And what about you going on TV, then, Jessica? You need to look good to be on telly, like that girl there,' and she pointed to Lisa Singh, who was wearing what looked like lots of old newspapers, but was actually the height of fashion.

Jessica had a strong urge to punch Agapanthus hard on the nose, but she resisted. This was no time to get into a scrap. Agapanthus would soon be smiling on the other side of her face: Jessica was going on TV, and how she dressed had nothing to do with it! In fact, Jessica *was* glad now there had been no time to go out and buy trendy clothes or do something to her hair. She didn't need any of that. All her earlier doubts were forgotten. She would show everybody!

'Ah, there you are!' It was Mr Flotsam, looking a little strange, with his usually shiny head all white and floury. 'I was wondering where you had got to, Xandra. You're to come with me, up onto the platform. I'm to make the introductions you know.'

'Oh really?' Xandra simpered and began patting her hair. 'I didn't realise that *I* would be appearing on TV too! But I might have known you'd arrange it, Bert.'

'It was nothing to do with me.' For a moment Mr Flotsam looked at Xandra with a strange expression on his face. Agapanthus, meanwhile, was smiling at Jessica smugly with a smile which said, clear as words, *my mother's going to be on TV and you're not.* She did not look so smug, however, when she heard what Mr Flotsam said next. 'Come along, Jessica. No, not you, Agapanthus. You can watch from here.'

Jessica grinned to herself at the sight of Agapanthus's face as she was left behind in the crowd, while Jessica and Xandra followed Mr Flotsam up onto the stage. A microphone had been set up, and Mr Flotsam tapped at it importantly. All the cameras were in place now, and Lisa Singh had finished her piece and gone back into the crowd.

She was standing near Bill Mycroft, who signalled at Mr Flotsam to begin.

'Hello everyone,' said Mr Flotsam. 'Greetings, and welcome to the grounds of Flotsam's Luxury Hotel – which, as you know, is the premier hotel in Bellstone, offering a luxurious and convenient home-from-home—'

Bill Mycroft gestured frantically, indicating that Mr Flotsam should get to the point. Mr Flotsam coughed and went on, 'Well, we all know why we are here today. We are all extremely proud of our local witch, Mellandra Haggerthwaite, and eager to see her make her historic attempt at human flight. But first Mrs Haggerthwaite's daughter, young Jessica Haggerthwaite, will say a few words.'

Jessica stepped forward. There was a pounding in her chest, and her hands felt sticky. In the moment before she spoke, she was aware of all the faces before her: Agapanthus, willing her to make a fool of herself; Bill and Lisa looking puzzled – they had not known she was going to speak; Sam Harris with his mouth wide open and Midge and Robbie both grinning and giving thumbs-up signs. She could see Clare, looking amazed, and even Miss Barnaby, beaming. Mr Flotsam kindly lowered the microphone for her, then stepped back.

'Ahem,' said Jessica. 'Good morning. I am afraid I

have an announcement to make. After a practice session earlier this week, during which she managed to stay suspended in the air for several moments –' (the crowd murmured, impressed) 'my mother, Mellandra Haggerthwaite, met with an unfortunate accident. I should add that the accident was nothing to do with flying.' (Well, it wasn't, thought Jessica. It was hitting the ground that caused the problems.) 'But due to her injuries, she will not be able to fly today.'

There were murmurings from the crowd. It seemed people did not know what to make of this. There were cries of 'Shame!' and 'Not Fair!' But others were more sympathetic. Jessica heard someone say, 'Well, if she's really hurt, poor love, you can't expect it', but someone else answered, 'It's all a con! She's lost her bottle.'

'Now wait a minute!' Xandra stepped forward and grabbed the microphone. She paused for a second, to rearrange her face from fury into her usual sweet, simpering expression. 'This really isn't on,' she cooed at the crowd. 'If people say they can do something, they should do it – shouldn't they? Otherwise they don't deserve to be believed. If I was one of Mrs Haggerthwaite's customers, I would know what to think. And I advise all her customers to leave her and consult me, instead.'

Jessica grinned. This was even better than she had hoped. 'Of course, everyone knows *you* can fly,' she said loudly. 'You proved it with that photo in the *Bellstone Gazette*.'

'Exactly,' said Xandra, batting her eyelashes at the camera. 'And I think Mrs Haggerthwaite should do the same. It's shocking of her to disappoint everybody like this. I mean, how do we know there's anything wrong with her?'

Clearly, several people in the crowd agreed with her. They began to shout indignantly, while Xandra stood smiling at them. Then a loud voice shouted, 'Make way! Make way there!' The TV cameras swung round to catch sight of Aunt Kate, waving the crowd apart like a policewoman. Behind her came Mrs Haggerthwaite. She was sitting in a wheelchair, being pushed by her husband, and wearing a long black dress and cloak, although these looked rather strange with one arm done up in a sling, and one leg all in plaster. She also looked very fed up – Mrs Haggerthwaite did not like people to feel sorry for her.

And sorry for her they were.

'Look at her, poor dear—'

'Broken every bone in her body—'

'Mad, I've always said it—'

'No, true dedication, that's what it is—'

Several people reached out and patted Mrs Haggerthwaite on her good arm, while others turned and cast extremely unfriendly looks at Xandra.

Xandra looked uncomfortable. She said 'Err' and she said 'Well', and then she tried to step back, away from the microphone. Jessica grabbed her arm, and spoke quickly to the crowd.

'Isn't it lucky, everybody, that we have here today, Xandra, Friend of the Wind Spirits! She's already told us she can fly. And she believes in proving things – she said so herself. So, I am delighted to announce that she will now give us an historic demonstration!'

The crowd cheered. After all, they had come here to see somebody fly, and they did not much care who. Although they were prepared to let Mrs Haggerthwaite off under the circumstances, they did not see why Xandra should not fly in her stead. She was plainly fit and well – and, as Jessica had pointed out, she had *said* she could fly.

Xandra went pale. Then her wrist twisted quickly in Jessica's hand, and she almost got away. But, to Jessica's surprise, Mr Flotsam stepped forward and grabbed Xandra's other arm.

'Come, my dear,' he boomed. 'Show them what you can do.'

'But Bert! I can't! I mean – I have to be in the right mood!'

'Then get into it!' A hard edge had entered Mr Flotsam's voice. 'You said in *my newspaper* that you could fly. So let's just see you do it!' His expression was not a nice one. It was the expression of someone who has successfully closed a hundred business deals, and got his own way every time. It was a shark-like, ruthless expression. Nevertheless, Jessica for one was extremely pleased to see it.

'But I don't fly off things!' Xandra bleated. 'I – I lift myself off the ground with the Spirits' help!'

'Good!' said Mr Flotsam. 'Do that, then.'

It was clear that he would not take no for an answer. Nor would the crowd, who were yelling 'Get on with it!' and 'We haven't got all day'. So, very reluctantly, Xandra lowered herself to the floor. She sat there with her legs crossed and her eyes shut tight. 'I call on the Spirits to raise me!' she cried. A tense silence followed. Everyone waited.

And waited.

And waited.

Xandra opened one eye. 'Err – I think maybe the Spirits aren't in the mood,' she said.

There was a brief pause. Then: 'Booo!' yelled the crowd. 'Hoaxer! Get her off!'

'I hope,' said Mr Flotsam in a nasty voice, 'this doesn't mean that you've been saying misleading things in my newspaper. That kind of thing could get the *Bellstone Gazette* into trouble. If that was the case, we might have to think about court action!'

Xandra did not stay to hear any more. She scrambled to her feet then, dodging both Jessica and Mr Flotsam, scuttled across the platform and into the crowd. A moment later, she disappeared into the trees with Agapanthus running behind her, and the jeers of the spectators following them.

Mr Flotsam looked as if he was going to go after her. But Jessica was no longer concerned with

Xandra and Agapanthus. The TV cameras were still rolling, but she knew it was only a matter of seconds before they stopped filming – once they thought the excitement was over. 'Wait!' she commanded the crowd in a loud voice. 'There is something still to see!'

The spectators fell silent. And somehow her air of authority held them, for they remained silent as they watched her march up the staircase that led to the scaffolding tower – a small figure, with brown curls blowing in the wind, and a determined chin. Then she knelt, and disappeared from view.

But the crowd waited, and the TV cameras remained trained upon the spot. What would she produce now? A magic carpet? A broomstick? Was she going to fly herself?

Up on the tower, Jessica experienced a

momentary feeling of doubt as she prised open the crate Midge and Robbie had left there. For a nasty moment, Archie stared up at her, looking no more friendly than usual. His beak was razor-sharp. But there was no time to waste. She took a deep breath, and grasped him firmly with both hands. She turned to face the crowd. For a second she forgot all about the TV cameras. All she was aware of were the trees, the birds singing in the branches, the glitter of the lake, and above everything, the vast expanse of sky. As a good scientist, Jessica knew that the earth's atmosphere was composed of oxygen and nitrogen. But at that moment it felt like something else altogether – something crafted from magic – a different, heavenly world.

It was Archie's world. So she raised him to the sky – and let him go.

Far below, Midge craned his neck to watch. He had agreed to this. He knew the time was right, and yet he had a strange lump in his throat.

There was a beating of wings, a storm of white, a swirling of feathers, as Archie discovered the strength in his newly mended wing. And then he was soaring through the air. For a moment, he wheeled above them, testing the air currents, while everybody watched, enraptured – then blinked as the sun made their eyes water. Then he was off, over the trees and out of sight.

Meanwhile Jessica had scrambled down to the platform and grabbed the microphone again. She looked around her. The crowd stared back at her, dazed.

'For years,' she began, speaking very clearly, 'human beings have wanted to fly. Science and magic have both tried to find ways – but they haven't found any, not without machines. Birds can fly. But, even though we are cleverer than birds, even though we make many wonderful inventions, we still can't fly the way birds can.'

She paused, glaring fiercely around her: at Mrs Haggerthwaite, who thought she could share nature's miracle with a mumbled charm and a handful of powder; at Mr Flotsam, who was in it for the money; and Bill Mycroft, who was in it for the viewing figures. Her expression softened. What she was going to say was what she had thought when she had first seen Archie, extending his wings and trying to lift off out of the Haggerthwaites' back garden. Now, she felt strangely shy about saying it. But she was going to, anyway.

'Human beings just can't fly! We think we can do everything – but we can't. But we can enjoy watching birds, who can. Instead of messing about, trying to fly, we should help to preserve birds, and take care of their habitats, so that they can fly for ever.'

She took a deep breath. 'This special Wilderness Garden is a marvellous place where all kinds of birds live.'

She signalled to Robbie and Midge, who were crouching almost out of sight at the back of the stage, holding the ropes that held the curtains in place. Next moment, the curtains and the big banner dropped away to reveal the Wilderness Garden, like a backdrop in a play: the lake glittering in the sun, trees with the wind rustling their leaves, drifts of wild flowers, foxgloves and daisies, patches of light and shade. It was as beautiful as ever – indeed, more so, thanks to the hard work of Mr Haggerthwaite. While everybody watched, a group of wild ducks, startled by the sudden fall of the curtains, rose from the water, their wings beating in perfect formation. A heron stared for a moment at the crowd, then turned and waded away.

A storm of clapping broke out. There was no doubt about it – Jessica's first TV appearance had been a huge success.

Chapter Eleven

There was a tremendous commotion everywhere: camera bulbs flashing, people chattering, the TV crew trying to dismantle their equipment; and a couple of dogs were fighting near the refreshment stand. Jessica, making her way through the turmoil in search of Midge and Robbie, found herself immediately collared by Bill Mycroft.

She really did not want to talk to him. She felt drained of energy and strangely light headed. All she wanted was to sit down and be very quiet for a few moments. But he did not give her much choice.

'A cracking performance,' he declared. 'Unusual, too. And you had them all right in your hand. Yes, I think this will make an excellent programme!'

Jessica listened as Bill Mycroft went waffling on

about how well she had done, when he thought the programme might be broadcast ('part of the autumn schedule, most likely') and what kind of payment she was likely to receive ('yes, there will be a nice little sum for you'). It was strange. A few days ago she would have been overjoyed to hear all this, but now she did not really care. Still, as he went on burbling, some of her excitement began to creep back. It was great that her plan had worked! And it would be gorgeous to get some money too. She would buy presents for everybody, she decided, including something especially nice for Midge, who would be missing Archie, and Mrs Haggerthwaite, who would be feeling miserable until her arm and leg healed. And if there was any left over, she would put it towards a computer. She had just about had enough of that old typewriter.

'– of course, we'll have to pad it out a little,' Bill was musing. 'Build on this idea of a Wilderness Garden. Maybe we can find a few celebrities with Wilderness Gardens – now there's a good idea.'

'What you should do,' interrupted Jessica firmly, 'is interview the man who does the gardening here. Then he can tell you how to make a habitat, and which kind of wildlife like what kinds of plants.'

'That's not a bad idea. Lisa can interview him – maybe he can find us some more wildlife to film.

Though, of course, it might be even better to find a well-known gardener, somebody the viewers have actually heard of—'

'There's no need for that,' said Jessica hastily. And she led Bill over at once to where Mr Haggerthwaite was standing, chatting with Mrs Haggerthwaite and Aunt Kate. Bill immediately began firing questions at him, and in a very short time, a rather nervous-looking Mr Haggerthwaite was standing in front of a camera while Lisa Singh quizzed him on the Wilderness Garden. He was rather hesitant to begin with but as he explained the importance of attracting more insects to the garden ('insects are what the birds eat, of course – you can't attract birds if you don't have insects') and extolled the virtues of daisies and buddleia ('a lot of people neglect these old-fashioned plants, but there's nothing like them for attracting butterflies'), all his nervousness disappeared. Jessica, watching happily, felt terribly proud of him. She wondered if *he* might be destined for TV stardom too.

Mrs Haggerthwaite was also happy. After all, her Incantation against Xandra had worked – even if it had taken longer than she had expected. The eyes of the people of Bellstone *had* been opened to Xandra's tricks. Lots of people kept coming up to Mrs Haggerthwaite to ask how she was doing, and to tell her they had always known that Xandra was a bad 'un (Mrs Haggerthwaite doubted this, but for once she had the sense to say nothing). A lot of them wanted to make appointments for consultations too.

Jessica saw all this and smiled to herself. Everything was turning out so well! But at that moment a heavy hand landed on her shoulder.

Turning around, Jessica saw that she had been congratulating herself too soon.

'Young lady,' boomed Mr Flotsam. 'I'd like a word with you. I have been doing some investigating.'

Robbie and Midge had escaped the crowds and were sitting by the lake eating cheese sandwiches and drinking lemonade, which Robbie had acquired in another raid on the hotel kitchens. Midge was alternately keeping an eye on Liverwort (necessary, with so many potential predators around) and staring out over the water, hopeful of spotting Archie. Robbie was wrapped up in his own thoughts.

'She's one of a kind, your sister,' observed Robbie after a while.

'Oh, she is,' agreed Midge, throwing his crust to a family of moorhens, and watching them paddle towards him across the lake.

'If she says she's going to do something, she does it,' Robbie continued.

'I suppose so,' said Midge. 'Most of the time.'

'My dad says he'll give her a job when she's older. He says that's what you need in business. Someone who gets things done.'

'She says she's going to be a scientist,' Midge pointed out.

'Yeah, well, I expect she will, if that's what she wants.' Robbie heaved a sigh and said, 'D'you think she'll come to the End of Term party with me?'

Midge, about to chuck another crust, froze; his hand remained suspended in midair. Then he stole a sideways look at Robbie, who was looking rather mournful and – well – *soppy*, Midge thought. He hadn't known Robbie Flotsam *could* look soppy. Mean – yes. Menacing – definitely. But soppy? He hadn't realised that was part of his facial repertoire.

'Dad's going to let me borrow a limousine from the hotel, and have one of the chauffeurs drive us there,' Robbie went on. 'But I don't know if Jessie will come.'

Midge boggled. Not only had Jessica become a full-blown Media Star at last, but it seemed that she was going to be a limousine-driven one – if she wanted to go to the party with Robbie Flotsam, of course. It was a very big *if*.

'I'll give you this advice,' said Midge kindly. 'If you do ask her – don't call her Jessie.' And he grinned to himself. Jessica liked a challenge. And Robbie Flotsam, gone totally soft on her – well, that would be a challenge of a new kind.

'Anyway,' said Robbie. 'I've got a treat for her—'

But before he could reveal what this might be, there was a crashing in the undergrowth, and Jessica herself appeared. 'Oh, there you are,' she said, plonking herself down beside them. 'I've been looking for you two.'

Midge grinned at her. 'We thought you might be giving a press conference. Or signing autographs for your adoring fans.'

'Ho, ho,' said Jessica. 'Listen, Robbie, I was just talking to your dad. And I don't think he's going to marry Xandra after all. He said he's been suspicious of her for a while. And when I told him what happened with the tape recorder at school – well, then he was *really* suspicious. He had one of his reporters at the *Bellstone Gazette* investigate her. They discovered that photo of her flying is a trick. They found out yesterday. That's why your dad was so keen to try and force her to fly today. He knew she was a con.

'And guess what – her real name isn't Xandra, Friend of the Wind Spirits. It's *Sandra Witherspoon*!'

'Hah!' said Robbie, in a splutter of crumbs.

'Yes, your dad reckons she's going to be leaving Bellstone, after what happened today. So we won't have to put up with Agapanthus at school either.' Jessica gave a contented yawn, then picked up Liverwort and tickled him with a frond of grass, in the way that he enjoyed. In her mind, she was typing up her notes that evening: the words spooled into her head like ticker-tape.

```
AIM: Become a TV star.
Done it!
AIM: Revenge on Xandra
Drummed her out of Bellstone, and that
revolting Agapanthus too!
AIM: Get Mum to Fly.
Well, didn't actually. But you can't
win them all. And we both had a real
good try.
```

Jessica stretched. 'Actually, it was a huge relief,' she told Robbie and Midge. 'When he came up and said he'd been investigating something, I was terrified he'd found out about us and that Spiritual Vortex!'

'Oh, he has,' said Robbie.

'What!' yelled Jessica. She and Midge both stared at Robbie in alarm.

'Yeah. He told me today that he put two and two together, and he reckons it was us who did it. But he's not that bothered.' Robbie grinned. 'Says we've a nerve, but he admires our spirit.'

'Well!' said Jessica. 'You never know, do you? I

thought he would call the police for sure.'

'So did I. But he says you've got to be ready for some underhand skulduggery in business. And he's glad we're showing some talent for it.'

'He would!'

'Also, I think some of the guests didn't like the Vortex. Told him it made the place look silly. I think he's secretly pleased we got rid of it for him.'

Jessica shook her head. 'I don't know,' she said.

'Anyway,' said Robbie, 'I reckon he's in a real good mood, even if he *has* just found out his girlfriend's a

swindler. Guess what, Jessie? He's getting me a brand new computer, when he puts in the new order for the hotel. And – and he says I can give you my old one.'

'What! But it's practically new!' In her amazement, Jessica did not even notice she had been called Jessie.

'I know.' Robbie grinned at her. 'He's not all bad, is he – my dad?'

And Jessica was forced to admit he was right.

Later that afternoon, Jessica and Midge sat together by the lake. The crowds had disappeared and Robbie had gone to find his dad. Jessica and Midge fed bits of bread to the mallards and moorhens, and enjoyed the sleepy warmth of the late afternoon sun.

'I hope Archie's all right,' said Midge suddenly.

Jessica looked at him with sympathy. 'He's probably heading for the sea, by now,' she said. 'Still,' she went on, 'everything worked out well in the end, didn't it?' And she rested her chin on her knees and watched the sunlight glinting on the water.

'Yes. It did.' Midge grinned at her suddenly. 'All right – I'll say it. You did it. You really are a Media Star!'

Jessica tried, and failed, to prevent a huge grin covering her face. 'It's a pity I won't see Agapanthus's face when my broadcast goes out.'

'You can't have everything,' said Midge.

'That's true. I didn't work out how Mum could fly, either.'

'But you turned it round,' said Midge. 'And it was nice what you said about birds. It surprised me.'

'It came into my head when I was watching Archie that time,' Jessica explained. 'I thought how he belonged in the sky and Mum – well, Mum didn't.'

'Yeah – some things science and magic can't ever achieve,' said Midge. 'You were right. Human beings can't do everything.'

There was a pause. Midge waited for Jessica to agree with him, and when she didn't, he looked at her suspiciously. Sure enough, her eyes were glinting in the determined way Midge knew all too well.

'I don't know about that,' said Jessica. 'You should never say never. Of course *magic* could never do something amazing like that. But *science*—'

'But you said—'

'Oh, I know what I said. And, of course, science doesn't know how to make Mum fly *now*. I found that out from all the research I did. But I've been thinking. We still don't know everything. People are making new inventions and discoveries all the time. Say some really good scientist, some time in the future – say they worked really hard at it and read lots of books, and did loads of experiments—' Midge let out a groan. 'Well, I don't see why I shouldn't,' said Jessica defiantly. 'One day. And then I'll get the Nobel Prize for sure! I'll be the most famous scientist in the world!'

Midge shook his head. He might have known. Jessica *never* gave up. Not for long. But at least if she was going to wait until she was grown up he didn't have to worry about it for the moment. And after all, you never knew. She might even succeed.

Then he saw something that put the whole matter out of his head. He leapt to his feet.

'Hey! Look!'

Jessica turned around. 'It's Archie!'

They watched as he came circling down towards the lake, looping and banking, before skimming across the surface in a great arc of spray. Midge and Jessica grinned at each other. It was a perfect end to a very satisfactory day.